Justice is Served

M. W. Leeming

Paperback: ISBN 978-1-913359-14-0
ebook: ISBN 978-1-913359-15-7

Book design by: Ian Sharman

www.markosia.com

First Edition

Nathan O'Hagan, Nick Quantrill.
Cheers, fellas.

'It is better to risk sparing a guilty person,
than to risk condemning an innocent one'
– Voltaire

The boy is ten. His stepfather, Frank, is chasing him with a length of stinging-nettle ripped from the overgrown borders at the back end of the garden. There's a vague sense of excitement in the boy: he knows that getting Frank riled up will always result in a chase. But the fear he feels comes from knowing that when he is caught, Frank will make him pay. And although the boy doesn't know for sure whether Frank really understands the nature of his condition, he still knows he'll end up in tears. Because Frank has that look on his face again. The look of a maniac in a third-rate teen-slasher.

And the boy knows this look.

But he's out of breath. His feet are slipping on the damp grass. He knows he'll soon fall, or give up and accept what's coming. Frank is a keen sportsman and could keep this up for hours.

The chase is up for sure when he feels the whipping of nettle on his bare calves. He doesn't feel any pain, of course. Just the contact of the tough stalk. But he decides to accept his fate. To slow down and let Frank rugby-tackle him. From here, Frank works in silence. Glaring at the boy with those psycho eyes. Holding his hands down. He kneels, and then straddles the boy, who tries to kick back, but it's useless. His legs aren't long enough. Frank pins him down tightly. Staring. Those psycho eyes.

The boy is frightened. He looks around for something he could use as a weapon. Something to get Frank off him. The only thing he sees is the gun-like nozzle of the garden hose, which is not within reach.

But Frank sees it too.

He clamps the boy's wrists into one big hand. Reaches out, and grabs the hose. The boy suddenly thinks that Frank may screw this up. That he can't possibly hold two writhing arms in one hand.

But no...

Frank is strong, and the boy's hopes are quickly dashed as Frank dangles the nozzle in front of his face, taunting him with a sadistic smile. Then he presses the nozzle to the boy's mouth.

The boy squeezes his lips tightly together. His panicked breathing rushing in and out through his nose.

Frank shuffles around some more. Readjusting his position. He presses down with his knees on the boy's arms, keeping the child pinned down and regaining the use of his hands. The boy feels pressure, but nothing else. Then Frank pinches the boy's nostrils shut.

A few seconds pass. Then a few more, as the boy holds his breath for as long as he can. He makes about twenty seconds. Until his senses scream for air, and his need is just too much. He opens his mouth and inhales with a loud, desperate gasp.

In that moment, Frank shoves the nozzle into the boy's mouth and squeezes the trigger. Cold water gushes in and the boy begins to thrash around. The water froths and churns in the back of his throat. He tries to insist that he's choking. That he can barely breathe. That he thinks he's going to die. And he *does* indeed think that Frank may really kill him this time.

But Frank doesn't listen. He keeps the boy's nostrils pinched. The water flow going. And the boy starts to panic.

This is it; he thinks.

And just when it seems he can't take any more, Frank suddenly cuts off the water flow and gets up. Satisfied. The boy has been put in his place.

The boy gets up, soaking wet. There are tears in his eyes. Anger and shame.

Frank has now regained the look of sanity, and he looks the boy up and down, shaking his head. Walks away in disgust.

The boy adjusts his grass-stained clothing. He looks at the house, and he can see into the kitchen where his mother has been preparing the evening meal. She was watching through the kitchen window the whole time.

Their eyes meet. And when she turns away with a shrug of the shoulders, he recognises the shame in her eyes.

If he thought for one moment that it was shame at Frank's behaviour, the boy might have felt reassured.

But he knows better.

Part One

Justice is Served

One

I had this client.

Reginald Chesterfield was a seventy-five-year-old man who worked as a department store Santa every Christmas. With no previous, he'd sailed through the CRB checks and bagged himself the job with ease. And Christ… he *looked* the part, too. White hair, white beard, half-moon glasses.

A few weeks ago, he took his laptop in for repairs. Whilst it was being examined, the repairman stumbled upon some images of children. The really bad kind. As a department store Santa, it was a terrible revelation.

When I first represented him, he fed me a total bunch of crap. This terrible stuff was research for a book he was planning, he said. I advised him that it might help to inform the police of this during his interview. It would establish his argument at the earliest opportunity, if nothing else.

The police then bailed him for a CPS review.

But really, there was nothing that would prevent Reginald from being charged. He had over a thousand of those disgusting fucking pictures and I knew what the CPS advice would be. When I went back for the bail-return, the officer confirmed it. After telling Reginald the news, he looked at me over his half-moon specs and whispered, "That copper doesn't like me much, does he?"

It freaked me out.

* * *

I was glad to be walking away from the police station after that. Glad to be out of the custody suite. No matter how often I saw the dour-faced cleaning ladies scrubbing the place down, I always left feeling sickened by the invisible filth of junkies, alcoholics and other degenerate wasters. I carried anti-bacterial hand-cleanser and squirted big dollops of the stuff in my palm, rubbing my hands together furiously as I headed back to my car.

Once inside, I sat behind the steering wheel, thinking for a while.

Reginald was a lost cause. He *deserved* prison. No two ways about it. And he'd never work as Santa again, that was for sure. He'd buckled under the strain of his rotten sexual perversions, feeding the industry of so-called 'child porn', and he should never be allowed to forget it.

But someone like him wouldn't be able to handle prison brutality. If he was convicted and sent down, I was pretty sure the guards would find him hanging one morning. And it was a thought that pleased me.

With that, I put the car into gear and drove off. I didn't know what I had waiting for me back in the office, but it didn't matter. The resentment for my work had started some time ago, and days like this didn't help at all.

* * *

Whenever I got back to the office after a police station call-out, my first port of call was Carol's room. There, my secretary would thrust at me a stack of all the telephone messages she'd taken in my absence. As I stepped into her room, she looked up at me from behind her desk, her phone propped against her ear by a raised shoulder. She scribbled notes with one hand, and passed me a thick wad of telephone messages with the other, eyebrows raised as though chiding me for not being in the office to take the calls instead, and putting her to incredible inconvenience.

I stood in front of her desk for a moment, sifting through the pile. Most of it was the usual stuff. Stressed out clients demanding updates, police officers reporting extended bail-returns, barristers chasing missing papers from trial briefs. But among all the shite, there was one that made my guts suddenly turn.

I hadn't spoken to Mum in years.

Why had she phoned the office?

I crumpled the message in my fist as I turned and walked upstairs to my office.

* * *

This is me aged eight:

I'm sitting alone at the dinner table eating my fish fingers and chips. I don't really want to eat the peas, though, because I don't like peas. I feel a slight pang of guilt because Dad went to the trouble of making them for me and I don't want to make Dad feel bad. And anyway... he says 'Eat your greens' because your greens are good for you and make you strong and put hairs on your chest. I'm not really sure I want hairs on my chest, but I do want to be strong.

As I eat, I'm aware of my *smallness* in the room. Aware of the noises I make in the silence. Dad served my food up and took himself upstairs. If I listen carefully, I can hear him crying and it's because Mum left to live with Frank and it still upsets him. She doesn't love Dad anymore, and she said she didn't want me to live with her and Dad could have me. That probably means that she doesn't love me, either, because if she did, she'd surely want me to live with her. But it's okay. I don't really want to live with her because I don't like Frank, and besides... Dad makes me fish fingers and I like fish fingers. And he gives me peas to make me strong, even though I don't really like peas.

* * *

I closed my office door, dropped my briefcase beside my desk and sat down, staring at my phone. I was going to have to ring her. Phoning me at work was not something she'd normally do, so *something* was wrong.

I took a deep breath and reached for my phone. Punched in her number. She answered after just a couple of rings.

"Mum," I said. "It's me."

"Jack. Sorry to bother you at work. I just phoned to let you know your Gran passed away last night. I thought you'd want to know."

"Right," I said. "Thanks."

There was a pause. Several seconds of awkward silence. I heard her sigh.

"Is that all you have to say?" she said.

I closed my eyes again. "That's terrible news," I said.

"You *could* sound as though you mean it."

"I'm busy, Mum. Text me the funeral details. I'll see you there."

Before she said anything else, I hung up.

* * *

"There are things you're too young to understand, Jack. But you're not too young to understand that Frank makes your Mum happy."

At eight years old, I know that although I myself feel no pain, I'm capable of causing it in other people. And not just physical pain.

Gran sits at the breakfast table to the right of me, a mug of coffee in front of her. Her hands are laced together as she leans forward to get in close. I have a bowl of untouched porridge in front of me, and a glass of orange juice. I lean forward too, looking up into her face and listening to this familiar sermon. Every time she visits Mum and Frank, she finds an opportunity to sit me down and tell me these things.

She looks at me, nodding ever so slightly, reassuring herself perhaps, that her lesson is sinking in. She picks up her mug of coffee, lifts it to her lips but instantly puts it back down.

"And another thing…" she says, stabbing the table-top with her gnarled index finger. "Frank works hard. Earns a good living. Takes care of your Mum. Your Dad never did that. Only ever put himself first. Drifting from one job to another. Incapable of holding a good job, incapable of holding on to friendships. It's a wonder your Mum put up with it for as long as she did."

I look up at her and don't say anything.

"You get on with Frank, right? You like him?"

I think for a moment. I bite my lip, because I'm not sure whether to say what she wants to hear or whether to tell the truth.

"Well? You like him, don't you?" she says again.

"Not when he tries to hurt me," I say, looking back up at her.

Gran frowns. Leans back in her seat and sighs loudly. Then she leans forward again. "That's just his way of having fun with you, Jack. It's difficult for him. Stepfather to another man's child. He's just trying to figure out how to have a relationship with you. And anyway… he can't hurt you. You know that."

This is true. I've never been able to feel pain. Not like normal people. Frank realised there was something wrong with me one day when he put a five-pound note on the table and said, "If you can touch it, you can have it."

As I reached out a hand, he suddenly slammed one of those hard rubber-soled slippers down *WHACK!* on my fingers. Feeling nothing, I carried on until my hand was covering the note. In frustration, he walloped my hand two more times, total confusion all over his face. But I didn't let go of the fiver.

"Congenital analgesia," I heard Mum tell him later. "He's never been able to feel pain. It's been a major headache for me, over the years. He got it from *him*."

Dad was the same, so she meant Dad.

But Gran was wrong. She was wrong about Frank. He wasn't trying to have fun with me. He was trying to have fun at my expense.

* * *

The service was underway as I went crashing in through the double doors. Midway through the hymn, 'Morning Has Broken', the congregation turned, and momentarily, the singing trailed off into a chorus of mumbles. When they saw it was me, they turned to face the front again.

I'd arrived late on purpose, not wanting to run into either Mum or Frank. As I took position at the back, I glanced over to Mum, up at the front. She spared the briefest glance in return and promptly turned away. But not Frank. He lingered there, glaring at me over his shoulder, eyes drilling their hate into me, eyebrows raised. An arm wrapped supportively around my Mum.

(You're a fucking failure, Jack! I always said so!)

I ignored the screaming insinuations from his glare and picked up an Order of Service, grimacing at the photo of Gran on the front. An almost perfect resemblance to Mum. Then I glanced back to Frank. He was deep into the hymn again, his back to me, hugging Mum in tight and close.

The singing continued.

Gran didn't deserve my singing voice. Instead, I started playing with the words in my mind, fitting them in with the melody:

> *Moaning and croaking,*
> *Like the last breath (of),*
> *A cancer-man smoking,*
> *Rejoice in her death.*

After the hymn, everyone took their seats with a brief series of hushed shuffling sounds. The service proceeded with all the usual sycophantic bullshit. A wonderful woman, a beautiful soul. Oh, how she'll be missed. I watched distant family members and barely recognisable friends weeping and hugging. When the congregation finally stood to listen to Michael Jackson's 'You Are Not Alone' the coffin slid away. The curtains closed with an awkward squeaking and off she went with her express ticket to Hell.

* * *

I didn't cause a scene. I could have. I could have exploded into a drink-fuelled supernova of hate but I remained calm and slunk from the crematorium before anyone noticed, deciding to give the wake a wide berth.

A few days later, a large envelope landed on my doormat. I opened it and shook out the contents. There were two smaller envelopes inside, one which had 'Jack' written on the front in my Mum's handwriting, and one in my grandmother's.

I decided to open and read Mum's letter first:

Jack,

Your Grandmother left you some money and a letter (enclosed). We already know what your Gran left you, and we'll get a cheque to you before probate is settled, as I'm sure you'll be keen to get your hands on the money. Of course, Frank thinks you shouldn't get a penny, but who am I to challenge the wishes of your kind and ever-loving Grandmother?

Mum.

I sneered at it and opened Gran's. I wasn't really sure I wanted to. There was a sudden sickness in my guts. But curiosity got the better of me.

It said:

Dear Jack,
I let you down. I am sorry,
Gran.

A while after that, the cheque turned up. It was for fifty thousand pounds.

Two

I'd taken a few days off work, playing the part of a grieving grandson. Taking time off was the sort of thing that other people would do and I'd realised some time ago that often in life it's best to do what other people do. To *look* normal and fit in. In any event, my head was a mess. Tons of thoughts swirling around my mind, like the noisy rushing chaos of a tornado, not least of which was the money Gran had left me. The anger was still there; a bright fury that smouldered beneath the surface of my outward calm. But there was a massive sense of confusion, too.

Why would Gran do this? Why show no interest in me throughout my life, only to leave a grand gesture at death? Why hadn't she spoken up before?

At first, I'd been tempted to rip the cheque to pieces. It was all just another head-fuck and it felt as though all my old scars had been torn open again. But in the end, I kept it.

Fuck it, I thought. And when you're talking about fifty thousand pounds, most people probably would have done the same.

* * *

Returning to work was grim. There was nothing else going on to save me from the backlog of dreary paperwork but it was impossible to make any progress. My secretary pumped incoming calls through to me, one after another. Refusing to filter them like a good secretary was meant to. A queue of frustrated callers who'd been waiting for me to return, impatient and in need of the peace of mind that I just wasn't interested in giving them.

I booted up my PC and perused the day's news. Headed to the website of the city rag and immediately felt sickened.

The Tooth Fairy had struck again.

A family of three, brutally murdered in the early hours of the morning. Lance and Janice Wendle. Ten-year-old son Jeff. Found by a neighbour, tied to their own kitchen chairs, they'd been bludgeoned to death. Special care had been taken to smash their teeth out and each victim was found sitting on a one pound coin.

Someone had labelled this sick bastard The Tooth Fairy after the first family were killed, several months back. It wasn't really hard to figure out why. There was a very clear echo of Thomas Harris's serial-killer in *Red Dragon*. Some weird fucker breaking into people's homes at night. Murdering entire families. Having some nicknamed monstrosity the focus of attention probably proved the morbid viewpoint that terrible news sells.

It made me want to puke.

Robert even joked that he hoped he was on duty the day The Tooth Fairy fucked up and got caught. A good earner, he'd said.

The idiot.

* * *

Robert had the gift of the gab. He could schmooze our clients and sweet-talk the magistrates. He was loud and domineering and knew all the right things to say to endear himself to anyone who didn't have to spend significant amounts of time with him. He'd trained me up well, and I couldn't really argue with that. But his grasp of law was pretty piss poor; he frequently had me confirm his theories with my fastidious recollection of very obscure points of law or, failing that, some speedy research to arm him with the required legal authority. And as far as the job went, we had a fairly efficient system going for a while.

But I'd long since been losing interest. It was a conflict, if anything. A conflict of moral priorities.

History is riddled with injustice. People convicted of crimes they didn't commit. Imprisoned for lengthy terms when innocent. People subjected to police misconduct. Evidence planted, hidden or contaminated. Judges sentencing excessively. It's all there. Lawyers help prevent it happening. And trust me, when it's happening to *you* it fucking matters.

Some people don't appear to care whether the guilty are punished too severely. They say things like: *How can you represent someone you know is guilty?*

The answer is simple: I don't *know* someone is guilty unless they tell me. But even then, the system still allows you to give a guilty person legal advice.

It works like this: I may have had my suspicions that a shoplifter was lying to me when he said that at the time of stuffing his pockets full of disposable razors, he had no intention of stealing them. That his basket was full and he definitely intended to produce them for payment. That he got distracted because his mobile went off with a call from his girlfriend to say his son was ill.

I may have *believed* that this was bullshit, and that when the shoplifter promptly went dashing from the shop with several pounds' worth of top-of-the-range razors bulging in his large overcoat, he fully intended to steal them. But my belief was not relevant.

Evidence is the key to proving someone's guilt.

Sure, I could point to the strength of the prosecution evidence and the likelihood of his acquittal in the face of it. But if this guy maintained his position that he did not intend to steal the razors, I had to go with that.

The problems start when you compare *actual* justice with *perceived* justice.

Robert once won a bail application for some ex-smackhead charged with burglary after she broke into her ex-boyfriend's house to steal his toothbrush. I don't know why she wanted his fucking toothbrush… she already had a dismal history of mental health problems, and I think she'd pretty much lost it the day they broke up. Robert latched on to the sympathy vote and managed to convince the court to release her. Later that same day, she went straight back to her ex-boyfriend's and stabbed him to death.

Robert agonised over that. Seriously. It kept him up at night. He thought he might have indirectly *caused* the death of the poor young man. And Lord knows, she wouldn't have been back out on the streets had it not been for his bail application. But he eventually came to the conclusion that he'd simply been doing his job. He didn't know what she was planning. There was no way he *could* have known. Any other lawyer would have done the same thing. The court had accepted Robert's argument that she was safe enough to walk the streets, and they had no reason not to; he hadn't *lied* to them. He was simply acting on the information available to him.

But still… it left a bad taste in the mouth knowing that when she was released, she freaked out and killed a man.

In terms of perceived justice, there hadn't been any. And this ought to have been enough to rattle the foundations of any criminal lawyer's moral boundaries. But there's no shortage of lawyers out there willing to do unethical things for their clients. Lying, producing false witnesses, becoming selectively deaf to awkward instructions. Some lawyers just didn't give a toss as long as they were known for never losing. What they cared about was keeping the clients rolling in.

I knew plenty of lawyers with a reputation like this, and I even lost some of my own clients to them. Tempted away by the promise of a miracle that would get them acquitted.

So, here was my problem. As far as perceived justice was concerned, I was in a very unique position. I had access to a lot of confidential information. I knew only too well that criminals were getting away with their scumbag behaviour.

* * *

My last job of the day was to prepare a brief for a Crown Court plea-hearing on a serious assault case. I stayed and saw the brief off myself. Then I locked up the office, got in my car, and drove off. I couldn't face the thought of cooking, so I called in at a McDonald's Drive-Thru and ordered a quarter-pounder meal.

As I sat in the car eating my burger, I watched the autumnal darkness seeping slowly into the sky.

* * *

I could see in my rear-view mirror just one other car, and I didn't think anything of it. I wasn't even sure how long I'd been distracted by my own thoughts, so I was taken by surprise when suddenly there was a knock on the glass of my driver's side window.

A hooded youth was standing there, bending slightly to look in at me. Gesturing for me to wind my window down.

I wound it down halfway.

"All right, mate," he said. "Got a light?"

"Sorry," I said. "I don't smoke."

The youth glanced around. "Never mind," he said. "I'll just take your wallet and phone instead."

It didn't register at first. The conversational way he'd said it threw me off guard. But when I saw him produce a knife, I realised what was happening. I knew this wasn't going to pan out well, but I wouldn't go down without a fight.

"No," I said. "I don't think so."

A look crossed the kid's face. A momentary confusion. He was probably all too used to terrorising people into getting what he wanted. But then he snapped and lunged for the car door. Yanking on it forcefully. I got the window up quickly and within seconds, his two mates were there, one on the passenger side and one at the front. They started kicking and punching the car, yelling at me to get the fuck out. I tried to start the engine but the yob on my side was punching the window too, again and again and again. Before I could turn the key, the window suddenly exploded, spraying fragments of glass all over me.

The next thing I knew, the guy was reaching in, grabbing for me. I instinctively threw myself into some kind of thrashing fit, desperately trying to fight him off but he leaned away from my flailing arms and his hands wormed their way further in.

That was when I realised I wasn't wearing my seatbelt.

His mates dashed round to my side, whooping with joy. With his hands now hooked beneath my armpits, he began to yank me out of the driver's seat and through the car window. His mates all got their hands in, helping him drag me from the car in several heaving tugs. I crashed to the ground with a thump, aware of the fact that although feeling no pain, the damage that could be done to my body was still very real.

The three of them were suddenly kicking me in the gut, chest, back and head. Over and over the blows came, and they were painless, but they were disorientating. I managed to grab the main youth's legs, and with a sudden yank, pulled them out from under him. He fell on his arse with a grunt, dropped his knife and I reached for it. He scrambled to his feet at the same time I did and I thrust the knife at him.

All three backed off.

"You *still* want my stuff?" I said, wiping blood from my nose with the back of my other hand.

"Fuck you!" said the ring-leader.

"Get moving," I said, thrusting the knife again.

The main youth rounded up his mates with one gesture and the three of them retreated back to their car. They never let me from their sight. There were a few half-arsed gestures egging me back on. An attempt to retain their idea of dignity, I suppose. They were not willing to show their fear. If I'd gone at them then, I'm pretty sure they'd have suddenly run for it. But they slunk back to their car anyway. The main youth started the engine; the car lurched forwards and screeched off out the car park.

His mates were giving me the 'wanker' sign.

* * *

I threw the knife down. Already, my mind was thinking about evidence. The knife may have had prints on it. I glanced around to see whether there were any CCTV cameras and there were.

McDonald's had been pretty empty, which was unusual. Just one family in the restaurant. But the incident had been so damn quick that it hadn't drawn any attention. I walked through the doors into the bright, glaring florescence of the restaurant and up to the counter. An acne-riddled teenager approached me, and I clocked his look of good cheer melting into horror like a hot waxwork dummy.

"Mate, are you okay?" he asked.

"Phone the police," I said. "I've just had the shit kicked out of me."

Three

The police took me to hospital with a broken rib and some bruising, but I was fine. I caused some excitement on the A&E ward. No one believed I couldn't feel pain. When it was clear I wasn't lying, I was visited by several doctors who wanted to shake my hand. Ask me questions. I was the freak show. The type of rare case they read about, but never saw up close. And with no further treatment necessary, I was soon discharged. Sent back home.

I phoned Robert the next morning and explained I was going to have to stay off work again. My rib needed to heal. And because I couldn't feel pain, I wouldn't know if I was doing anything to hamper this.

He wasn't impressed.

"We've got a ton of work on, Jack," he said. "This is a bad time. You just had time off for the funeral!"

"I'm sorry," I said.

"Don't take too long," he said, and slammed the phone down.

Later, I had a visit from the police. The officer was PC Rachel Slater. She sat down with her pocket notebook, flipped through the pages and sighed. I knew her from previous dealings in custody. I'd always liked her, to be honest. Not only was she good-looking, she was a good copper. Firm and focused on the one hand, caring and compassionate on the other.

Her radio was intermittently jabbering away, and she turned the volume down a touch.

"All right," she said. "I haven't got good news, I'm afraid."

I knew instantly where this was going.

"We examined the CCTV at McDonald's. Unfortunately, it didn't capture anything of the incident. It was looking in the wrong direction. We spoke to several members of staff that were on duty at the time. None of them witnessed the attack."

"What about the family in the restaurant?"

"My colleague spoke to the mother and father last night," said PC Slater. "They *think* they may have heard something, but are refusing to make a statement. Like a lot of people, they're probably too scared. They don't want to get involved."

I nodded. "Any prints on the knife?"

"Nothing," she said, and I sensed remorse in her voice. "I'm so sorry."

I offered her a smile. "It's not your fault."

"Do you believe in karma?" she said.

"I do," I lied, just for the sake of politeness.

"Me too," she said, smiling. "What goes around comes around, eh?"

I smiled back.

And then the silence fell. It was only momentary, but within that silence there was suddenly a great deal to be understood. PC Slater looked at me with a compassion that was more than just sympathy. I had long been hiding my feelings of attraction to her, and in that moment I suddenly sensed that she felt the same. *That* locking of eyes, *that* trembling excitement, *those* butterflies in the stomach. The mutual knowledge which seems somehow to exchange within a lingering glance, like a psychic communication.

With a sudden look of embarrassment, she stood and tucked away her notebook. "I've got to go," she said, and the link was broken.

She headed for my front door and I followed, to see her out.

"Thank you," I said. "Thanks for everything you've done."

She looked me in the eye again. It didn't quite re-establish that link, but certainly acknowledged its previous existence. "I'm sorry we couldn't get them for you, Jack. If you need *anything*, ring me. I mean it."

She handed me a card. On the back, she had written her mobile number and her name, and our eye contact remained fixed as I took the card.

"Sure," I said.

And then she left.

* * *

Strange thoughts and weird dreams. I awoke in the night screaming, scenes from a dream still floating before my mind's eye like flash-bulb after-images.

Frank was chasing me. Shouting at me that if I didn't stay still and get my treatment, I'd be on Santa's Naughty List.

There were fragments of a song, echoing from a distant gramophone:

Deck my balls with boughs of holly,
Fa la la-la-la la la-la laaaa!
To make them bleed it makes me jolly,
Fa la la-la-la la la-la, laaaa!

I didn't remember the rest, and didn't fucking want to.

* * *

It was eleven by the time I was up, showered and dressed. I ate toast with Marmite and drank a strong coffee. I had a hospital appointment later, to check on my ribs. Not that there was anything they could do. I didn't even need any painkillers. But because of the absence of pain, the doctors wanted to get a sense of how it was healing. How quickly I could return to work.

Sitting in my lounge with the coffee, I played distractedly with the card PC Slater had left me, deep in thought.

I'd been thinking about her visit. Wondering about that moment. Whether it was just wishful thinking. Whether in fact there had even *been* a moment. Whether I was just reading too much into an awkward silence.

But why had she left her card? Had it been because she *wanted* me to phone her? To ask her out? Or was it because she was extending me a support network? A sympathetic ear.

One thing was certain, though, and that was with every hour that put distance between now and *then,* I wasn't so certain. I put her card on my mantelpiece. I'd talked myself out of ringing her but I didn't want to dispose of it.

Optimistic?

Perhaps not. The beating at the hands of those bastards left me angry. Disheartened and hateful. But it was more than that. People like them always seemed to get away with it. Christ... I was one of the fucking idiots that helped them. Why did it seem that some people were just destined to be life's victims? The weaker offerings of human evolution? Why did those fuckers target *me?* What was it about me that gave them the impression I could've been fucked over so easily?

Fucking people... They were nasty, vicious and greedy. The world of morality was a different thing for people like that. They were happy with the idea of smashing up my face to get what they wanted. Their world was an animal kingdom of simple wisdoms.

But no… It was worse than animal. If a lion killed an antelope, it was survival. Not because the antelope called its mother a whore.

People were varied and complicated and yet so fucking stupid on *many* different levels. But it was always the bigger, stronger and nastier bastards lashing out and imposing their will on those with smaller, weaker and kinder dispositions. Did they have something to prove, or something to gain? The pursuit of power, combined with savage thuggery and poorly considered moral codes. Life was a constant battle of wills. On the streets, it was gangs, drugs, turf. Strike, counter-strike. Action, revenge. In business it was ambition, money, power. But there was little difference. The common thread was Big overpowering Small.

Life would remain a miserable conflict until people realised the futility of it all. Until people understood that the right to trample others for their own self-serving purposes was a right that no-one gave them but themselves. And it wasn't therefore a right, but a personal justification for being a nasty cunt.

It was making me angry.

I clenched and unclenched my fists. Casting my mind back further.

* * *

That bastard, Frank. When I was a kid, he would shut me in the cellar and turn the lights off. He would laugh as I cried and bawled and thumped on the door, pleading to be let out. He'd laugh as I became hysterical with fear.

There was something wrong with that fucker and no mistake. Forbidding me from helping myself to food from the kitchen cupboards. Going mad at meal times when I left waste. He didn't give me the whole *starving-children-in-Africa* spiel, though. It was always about how his money paid for the food that was going in the bin, how bins got emptied into a landfill, how landfills were plagued by scavenging birds and how birds would shit on his expensive suits.

"Those bastards are eating *my* hard-earned money and shitting it back all over me," he would say. "So finish your damn meal."

He once got drunk and touched a red-hot iron to the bare skin of my upper arm, his face lit up with a great big smile. I never felt it, and to him it was just another funny experiment. But Mum made me promise never to tell Dad about it afterwards and I didn't.

Remembering these terrible things, I was bound to start feeling bad.

I was *bound* to.

* * *

Robert was on duty when I returned. Flustered, and stressed out.

"Thank God you're back," he said as I came through the front door. "I'm going to need you to cover me."

"Okay," I said.

"I'll get the call centre to put the calls directly through to you. That'll free me up for court. Okay?"

"Okay," I said.

"Hopefully you'll bag that Tooth Fairy nutter, eh!" Robert grinned at me, before swallowing the dregs of his coffee, collecting his files for the day and sweeping out of the building like a fat whirlwind.

I looked at Harry and shook my head in despair. He was sitting down and sipping tea. Calmly browsing a file on the desk in front of him.

"Ignore him," he said. "How you doing?"

"Not too bad," I said. "Thanks."

Harry nodded. "Just try and take it easy."

I smiled back, politely.

* * *

It was a quiet rota but a call came in at lunch. Some little prick was being held for robbery. A street-mugging by the sound of it. I took the preliminary details from the call-centre, then phoned the custody suite at my local nick. The sergeant gave me some more information and advised me that the officer-in-charge would be ready for interview in an hour.

I rolled up in good time.

"Hello, Mr Jones," said Sgt Hardwick from behind the custody desk. "You're here for Leon Hunt?"

"I am. Can I take a look at his custody record, please?"

The custody record provides personal details, information about the arrest and compliance with legal obligations. Always a handy starting point for the lawyer. When I'd finished examining it, I passed the record back to Sgt Hardwick and asked to speak to the officer-in-charge.

"That's fine," said Sgt Hardwick. "The officer is PC Slater. Take a seat in a side room, and I'll get her down for disclosure."

"Thank you," I said, gathering my things and walking around the custody desk to an interview room.

As I sat waiting, I felt a heat in my guts. Anxiety. Excitement. I couldn't believe my luck. How would PC Slater react when she saw me? Would the attraction still be there? Would we both sense it again? Would it interfere in my objectivity?

The anticipation was exhilarating and yet also rather unsettling. I desperately wanted to see her again, but not here. Not like this. Our professionalism would prevent a discussion even remotely hinting at our feelings. But I was overwhelmed with the desire to see her all the same.

And then she came in.

* * *

"Hello, Mr Jones," she said, smiling.

She was in plain clothes and her hair was down. I was aware of her perfume, something I had never really noticed before. A delicate fragrance, light and flowery. I noticed a touch of make-up. Was this for me?

But her tone. It didn't reveal any pleasure in seeing me at all. It was business-like and formal.

"Hello, officer," I said. I tried to sound as neutral as I could.

PC Slater took a seat opposite me at the interview table. She had a folder of notes and witness statements.

"How are you?" she said.

I nodded. "I'm good, thanks. Back here, at any rate."

"Glad to hear it," she said. Her eye contact was unreadable. I sensed nothing. "So, you're here for Mr Hunt, eh?"

"I am," I said. "What have you got?"

PC Slater briefed me. In the early hours of the morning, CCTV picked up a young man staggering down Booze Alley, a well-known cluster of city pubs and bars. This was the victim. He was drunk, and heading for a taxi-rank when another man approached him and asked for the time. As the victim checked his watch, the other man punched him several times to the head, knocking him to the ground. The man bent down, rummaged through the pockets of the semi-conscious victim and removed his wallet. He ran off in the direction of the railway station, where he was arrested by police officers alerted by the CCTV operator. CCTV images were unclear. But it didn't matter. Leon was searched and found with the victim's wallet on him, which contained about a hundred pounds in twenties.

The victim had provided an initial statement, and although his memory of the incident was foggy, he was able to provide a fairly good description. He had minor cuts and bruises but was more shaken by the incident than injured. He also said that he'd seen the suspect around town before, and knew he had some dangerous friends. He was pretty scared about the repercussions of making a complaint, and some doubt existed as to whether he was going to see it through.

So far, Leon had said nothing to the police. He obviously knew he was fucked, and had called for the duty solicitor because he wanted to know *exactly* how fucked he was. He had previous, but nothing substantial.

I thanked PC Slater and asked for a consultation with him. She said she would fetch him from his cell, and bring him to a consultation room further down the corridor. I watched her leave the interview room, trying to guess her thoughts but I couldn't, and gave up.

Leon truly was fucked. CCTV had captured the robbery, then followed him from the scene. He had the victim's wallet on him at the time of arrest. The only issue was the victim's willingness to see this through. It was a definite no-comment job, I knew that much.

I went and waited in the consultation room. Got out my notes, and within a few minutes the door to the room opened. I had my back to it. I preferred to sit this way for a quick escape in case some violent bastard took a dislike to me one day.

I heard PC Slater say, "Leon, this is your solicitor, Mr Jones." Then she was gone, closing the door behind her.

Hunt slumped into the seat opposite me, stinking of sweaty socks and armpits. My notes were spread out on the table between us, and I looked up from them.

I recognised him instantly.

* * *

"So, what they got on me then?"

His hangover voice was a rough croak and his breath smelled like a dog-shit sandwich. I'd experienced this a million times before. But *his* voice stabbed sudden anger through my brain. It was the same voice that had asked for my wallet and phone. The voice which had belonged to the youth who'd dragged me from my own car and kicked me all to hell.

And he didn't even recognise me, the bastard.

I cleared my throat. Discretely reached for the call-button next to my seat and pressed it. Summoning a member of custody staff to come and let me out. They'd wonder why, of course. Why I wanted out so soon. But it was none of their business.

"Come on," he said. "What they got?"

"Something has just come to my attention," I said. "You're going to have to go back to your cell."

There was a knock on the door. I quickly gathered my shit together, picked up my briefcase and moved for the door. When I opened it, the jailer was stood there, and I indicated to Hunt. "Can you take him back, please? I have to take care of something."

"Of course," said the jailer. "Come on, Leon."

He stood up. "What the fuck's going on?"

"All in good time," said the jailer. "Let's go."

Hunt left the room. He glared at me as he went. The jailer led him to his cell and I heard his voice echoing down the corridor. "What's that bloke's fucking problem?"

The jailer told him to remove his shoes and I heard the cell door slam shut.

* * *

I was back before the custody desk, and Sgt Hardwick was scrutinising me with suspicion. Not a particularly unique experience.

"I'm going to have to withdraw from this case," I said to him.

Sgt Hardwick's eyebrows lifted. He knew he wasn't entitled to know the reason for my decision. But he asked anyway.

"Conflict of interests," I said. "This case will have to go to back-up. Can someone let me out, please?"

Back-up was a pain in the arse for the police, so far as I could tell. They were legally bound by a twenty-four-hour time limit to get their job done, and when things like this happened, they had to wait whilst a new lawyer was instructed. It was all just bureaucratic guff, eating into their time.

Sgt Hardwick sighed loudly, clearly frustrated. "Yes," he said. He indicated to a jailer to send me on my way. I looked around, but PC Slater was nowhere to be seen.

* * *

That was the quietest duty in a long time and Robert was angry.

"What exactly *was* the conflict?" he said.

"He's a co-defendant in an existing matter we have," I lied. "Cut-throat defence. He's blaming our guy."

I knew Robert wouldn't have a clue what I was talking about. He didn't have a good memory for the details of our cases. Not like I did. So, he didn't bother pushing it.

"For Christ's sake!" he grumbled. "One case and we had to throw it away."

I clocked out at 5pm and drove home, thinking about Leon the whole way. I opened a beer and sat in my lounge. I wanted to think about Rachel but my mind wouldn't focus. It kept wandering back to Leon Hunt despite all my efforts to steer it towards something nicer.

I told myself that what he'd done to me hadn't been personal. That he existed within a framework of low-level moral values, and possessed poor intellectual abilities. I told myself that he may have had some mental impairment, or that he could have been under the influence of drink or drugs. I even told myself that he may have been under duress. But none of it mattered.

I'd had enough of this shit. I was going to get him.

Four

My main failing at work was my Paperwork Constipation: I had problems getting
it out.

There were times when I was on a manic roll. Still buzzing from a good result in
custody, I could rattle the paperwork out like Charles Dickens on speed. But that
was not very common. Usually, I put it off. Found something more interesting to
do. It always got to the point where Robert needed it done *yesterday*. He'd be yelling
at me, stressing out. Fearful of losing money on an out-of-date police station bill.
For that reason, most of my paperwork was completed in an agonising, mad rush
of almost-missed deadlines and tense moments of intolerable stress.

So, I still had the paperwork from my brief trip to the police station. Which
meant I knew where Leon Hunt lived.

* * *

I packed my rucksack with black gloves, a black scarf, a black baseball cap and a
roll of parcel tape. I went out to the car and unscrewed the number plates, threw
them in the boot and drove into the rougher outer-city streets. The concrete
wilderness. Round here, the years had been cruel. Everything had a hopeless feel
to it, and that was reflected in the fact that I had a large client base from this area.
Great towering flats rose ominously from the gloomy streets.

I drove around in the dark, searching for the address I'd memorised, passing several large groups of youths hanging around on street corners, smoking, drinking, yelling or fighting. After a while, I found it and parked the car on the opposite side of the road, a little further down. It seemed a bit quieter here. I looked at the house through my rear-view and considered my options.

Leon Hunt was twenty-years-old, and lived with his mother. I didn't know whether he had any siblings, so I couldn't risk entering the house for fear of being outnumbered. This made my task harder; I knew that. But I also knew that there had to be *something*. Some way of infiltrating his space.

And that was when everything resolved itself. Right place, right time.

The front door to his house opened and out stepped a woman with the skeletal face of a long-term junkie. All the life sucked out of it. Haggard and worn. She turned to look back into the house and I heard her as she shouted:

"Leon, I'm off out! Don't wait up!"

She shut the door, gathered her coat around her and walked off down the road, away from my car.

* * *

Okay, so this was Hunt's mother, and the shout had been addressed to Leon directly. He was alone.

She'd told him not to wait up, which probably meant she was going to be out late. I could have broken in quietly, but I ran the risk of being caught. Even if he bumped into me accidentally, he might get the advantage. So, I needed to bring him to me, and now that I knew he was alone, that would be easy.

I pulled out my gloves from the rucksack and put them on. Wrapped the scarf around the lower half of my face, covering my mouth and nose. Placed the baseball cap on my head and pulled it down low. I stuffed the roll of tape into my coat pocket. Got out of the car and left it unlocked for a quick getaway. I crossed the road, walked to the front door. Knocked, but not too urgently. I didn't want to raise his suspicions. I waited. Heard footsteps approach the door from inside. Then the mechanism of the latch.

And the door opened.

* * *

With a powerful kick, the door flew inwards and struck him in the face. He reeled back with a grunt and a grimace of pain. Tripped over some shoes lying in the hall and fell over. I stepped into the house and closed the door behind me. Quickly moved over to his fallen, slumped heap and removed the parcel tape from my pocket. I sat on his chest, pinning him down and moving as quickly as I could, wrapped the tape around his head, sealing his mouth shut.

I didn't need a concerned neighbour reacting to screams.

With several layers now wrapped around his face, I grabbed his arms. He was struggling. Fighting against it. Legs thrashing around, trying to kick me and wriggle out of my hold. But I had the advantage here.

Moving quickly and quietly, I bound his wrists and ankles. When I'd finished, I stood up and looked down at him. A wretched little maggot, squirming and writhing around in the hallway. Grunting noises from the back of his throat. Breathing heavily through his nostrils.

He was clearly terrified. His weasel-like eyes were now bulging from the sockets and he looked like that famous old horror movie actor Peter Laurie.

I rested for a moment. Gave myself time to think.

Justice was what I wanted, and it seemed important that what I do should be proportionate. Anything excessive was out.

I took stock of the injuries I'd been left with. A broken rib and several bruises.

I bent down and grabbed him under the arms. Dragged him from the hallway and into his lounge. There, I turned the main lights off and switched a lamp on.

I wasn't going to break a rib. I wasn't entirely sure how much force was needed to accomplish that. I couldn't be sure that I'd actually break one, or that I'd go overboard and break more. If I started laying into him in the same way he had me, I could have done some serious damage.

In the end, I decided to break his leg. It would be enough to hurt like a motherfucker, and it would be roughly proportionate to the injuries he'd given me. I didn't want him to get off *lightly*, but I also felt that a broken leg would do the job.

I picked up his tightly bound ankles, swung him round to face the sofa and propped his feet on the arm-rest. With a hefty stamp, I brought my boot down on his right shin. The crack was loud. His scream was trapped at the back of his throat, muffled by the tape over his mouth. There was no chance anyone heard it. But the bone busted badly. Blood seeped through his jeans where the break had clearly torn through the flesh of his leg. I thought about it briefly, decided I didn't mind but to leave it there and call it a job done.

As he squirmed around in muffled agony, I glanced around the room. On the coffee table – beneath a tin of tobacco, some rolling papers and an ashtray – was a police charge-sheet. I bent down to examine it and saw that it was Hunt's charge of robbery from earlier that day.

And then an idea came to mind. I searched for a pen. Tore a strip of paper from the charge-sheet and scribbled something on it in block capitals. I removed the roll of tape from my pocket, tore off a piece, and taped the note to his forehead.

After that, I left the house, went back to the car and drove home. I parked up, re-attached the number plates and went indoors, thinking about the note. It had been a moment of inspired creativity. The moment which would shape the things to come.

It said: *JUSTICE IS SERVED.*

Five

I kept an eye on the news. There was one feature about Hunt, but no more than that. It was only one paragraph in the paper. A brief summary that some masked assailant had forced his way into Leon's home, bound him in parcel tape and broke his leg.

It also mentioned that he was on bail following a robbery charge, and mentioned the note.

Justice is Served.

I didn't expect a full-scale police investigation. Leon Hunt was shit on their shoe, and only I knew that justice had been done for the attack I had suffered. Plus, there was this other robbery charge now. Nobody would care about a brainless thug like him. People would think he'd got what he deserved.

* * *

By Saturday, I was buzzing. Recharged with a brand-new confidence. I picked up Rachel Slater's card, ready to phone her. And I was going to do it, too. But before I could, my mobile rang.

The coincidence was spooky.

"Hello, Mr Jones," she said when I answered it.

"PC Slater?" The sound of surprise was clear in my voice. "What can I do for you?"

"Well," she said. "I suppose I ought to come out with it."

"Yes?"

"I've spent the past few days thinking about this, and I reached the conclusion last night that you were *not* going to ring me, even though I left you my number. I realised that I would be waiting forever if I left it to you. So, the obvious solution to this problem was to ring you myself and encourage you to ask me to dinner."

My belly suddenly filled with the fluttering intensity of excitement.

"Did you, indeed?" I said, keeping my cool.

"That's right."

There was a long pause as I thought my response through. A playful, teasing silence.

"Well in that case," I said, "would you care to join me for dinner tonight?"

"I don't know. I'll think about it."

And then she hung up. I stood there in surprise, looking at the phone. Had I done something wrong? Was she just fucking with me? I didn't know what I was meant to do, and just as I was starting to kick myself the phone rang again.

"Hello?"

"I've thought about it," said Rachel. "And I'd love to. I'll be there at seven."

She was gone again.

* * *

When seven came, I was a bag of nerves and to make it worse, Rachel was fifteen minutes late. For that dreadful quarter of an hour, I convinced myself she wasn't coming.

I'd been out and got some bits in for a meal. A few bottles of good wine. Had a tidy round, lit a few candles. Put on a CD which played softly in the lounge. The ambience was nice. But I was sick of pacing around, so I opened a bottle of red to calm my nerves. As I was pouring myself a glass, the doorbell went. I opened the front door with my glass in one hand. Nice and calm.

"Hello, Mr Jones," she said, smiling. She passed me a bottle of wine. "Started without me, eh?"

"Hello, officer," I said. "Come in."

As she walked into the house, she removed her coat and hung it on a peg in the hall. She looked nice.

"I would say I'm sorry I'm late," she said. "But that would be a lie. It was a carefully calculated manoeuvre."

I laughed. "That's fine. Come through to the kitchen and I'll get you a drink."

* * *

We made small talk for a while but there were very clear vibes of a gentle, flirty nature. After a while, I invited her to sit at the kitchen table. She took her glass of wine and sat down.

"What's on the menu?"

"Chef's specialty," I said. "Lasagne."

I served up. Placed toasted ciabatta into a basket and sat down opposite Rachel. I was careful not to overload the plates.

As she tucked in, Rachel said, "So why did you run out on me the other day?" She sipped her wine.

"Conflict of interests," I said. "I had to withdraw. I looked for you as I left, but you weren't around."

She smiled. "I was keeping an enigmatic distance."

"Really?" I said. "I thought you might have had something important to attend to."

"That *was* pretty important."

I smiled.

"Did you hear about our good friend Mr Hunt?" she asked.

I nodded. "I saw something in the paper."

"I've dealt with him before. He's a horrible little shit. It didn't really come as much of a surprise."

"Yeah. Live by the sword, and all that."

"Funny thing, though," she said. "That note."

Sudden waves of paranoia. "What do you make of it?" I said.

She shook her head. "It's not my investigation. But he obviously pissed someone off and paid the price. I don't see anyone crying into their soup over it though."

"Harsh," I said, "but true."

She smiled.

"So," I said, keen to change the subject without being too obvious. "Do your superiors know you're here?"

"Oh, yes," she said. "In fact, they're probably listening in right now. I'm wearing a wire."

I laughed, knowing it was her humour but at the same time anxious again. *Could* she have been wearing a wire? Could it be possible that this was all an act? Did she suspect me?

"Seriously, though," she went on. "What the hell has it got to do with *them*? My superiors *may* get an attack of the heebie-jeebies if they knew, but I'm a trusted and respected officer. If I choose to fraternise with the Dark Side, that's up to me."

* * *

After clearing away the plates, I served cheesecake. The meal was no culinary masterpiece, just something nice over which we could talk and drink and get to know each other. Later, we collected our glasses and a bottle of wine and moved through to the lounge.

"Very nice," said Rachel, looking around.

"You seemed to be worth the effort," I said. She laughed, and sat down.

We talked for a while, me on one sofa, her on the other. Eventually, Rachel told me that she was teaching herself to palm-read. She invited me to sit next to her on the sofa to give me a reading. I went over, sat down and she shuffled closer to me. I gave her my right hand, she turned it palm-up, and said:

"Just as I thought. Intelligent, but gullible."

I looked at her. "What?"

"Palm-reading is a load of rubbish," she said. "I just wanted you to sit over here."

With our physical space now close, the nature of our interactions were more personal. I turned to sit facing her – she sat cross-legged facing me. We discussed things on a more intimate level.

It was about 1am when Rachel looked at her watch and said it was getting late. That as much as she wanted to stay, she really had to make a move. I phoned a cab for her and we reverted back to small talk whilst waiting for it to honk from outside, and when it did, I escorted her to the door.

I was momentarily unsure whether to lean in for a kiss, but on balance, it seemed a little presumptuous. As if reading my mind, Rachel smiled at me and said, "No chance, Mr Jones. I have an enigmatic façade to maintain, remember."

"Of course, officer," I said, smiling.

"You may be luckier next time."

"There'll be a next time, then?"

She smiled back at me. "I've had a lovely evening. There will *definitely* be a next time," she said.

And with that, she gave me a gentle kiss on my cheek, turned and walked down the drive to the waiting cab.

* * *

After that, I couldn't sleep. Thoughts like a Formula One race-track.

Rachel was the first woman I shared a genuine connection with. I felt at ease in her company. Her sense of humour was abstract and I liked it. I was keen to spend more time with her. The paranoia I'd felt earlier was understandable. Rachel was an officer of the law. She believed in the administration of justice the way it was meant to be done.

But I couldn't help wondering: if it was true that she felt Leon Hunt got what he deserved, how would other people feel? Surely I wasn't the only one sick of criminals walking free. Society was in a mess. Incompetence and apathy were rife. People getting away with too much, punishments often inadequate. I knew this better than most. It just wasn't good enough anymore.

Something *had* to be done about it. Someone *had* to stand up, fight back.

As a concept, popularising vigilantes was an old one. From the tales of Robin Hood to America's present-day costumed crime-fighters and so-called 'Real Life Superheroes'. One way or another, people at the shitty end of the stick have long felt a deep-rooted need to fight against injustice and apathy, and to root for those doing it.

Hell, Phoenix Jones would agree with that!

And true, *some* do rely on faulty ideals. Greed for power. A mindless justification of ignorant beliefs. Racism, religion, misunderstanding. These can all lead to terrible and unpardonable things. Lynch mobs, vigilante groups driven by fear and ignorance and a willingness to fight and hurt.

I'd have to be careful. Because obviously, it wasn't going to be someone *like* me. It had to be *be* me.

It was time the guilty were punished the way *real* people thought they should be. Not high-and-mighty, wig-wearing toffs living out in the sticks somewhere, well away from the grit of *real* life.

Fuck that.

Comic books portrayed vigilantes favourably and as fiction, people bought into it in a big way. But often, these heroes had unique abilities or powers. I possessed no super-powers, of course, but I had a unique condition which could be put to good use. The advantage I had over the scumbags on the street was my inability to feel pain.

True, I had no training in martial arts. I couldn't sling webs from my wrists and stick to walls. I definitely didn't turn green when I was mad and I couldn't fly at the speed of sound. But I wasn't going to be dealing with super-villains boasting high IQs and mad plans to conquer the world. This would be morons on the street. Thugs. Arseholes. Perverts. My abilities were more in context with the brutal reality of everyday criminals.

I remembered I'd seen two very good movies recently. The first was *Kick-Ass*. The second was *Super,* a darker and certainly more unbalanced take on the normal-guy-goes-hero concept. They were good. They were great movies and, in truth, there were probably tons of people who would like to do this. To fight crime. To be a hero. But these were two films from which I could learn very little... except, maybe one thing.

The uprising of a vigilante would get a reaction.

* * *

Of course, I had to think it through. It had to be done right. And there'd be things I'd need. With fifty thousand pounds now sitting in my bank account, that shouldn't be a problem. I could get my hands on almost anything I needed from the internet. But I'd have to be careful; ensure that *nothing* led back to me. No paper trails.

The path I wanted to tread was a path considered criminal by the authorities. Not only would I expose myself to criminal sanctions, I would lose all credibility. A vigilante needed to rely on a sense of *menace*. Knowing it was plain old Jack Jones prowling around wouldn't work. I'd just be a fucking laughingstock.

But a secretive, faceless symbol of justice, intolerance and punishment... well; then a sinister and perilous vibe would prevail.

I started getting excited about the plan, and sat down with a beer at my kitchen table to brainstorm. To make a list of things I thought I'd need.

A good name, a costume, a vehicle. Weapons. Calling cards, maybe.

The *Justice is Served* thing from dealing with Leon Hunt struck me as a great way of leaving my mark. I began playing with ideas, and settled on one I liked. Black business cards. *Justice is Served* in white script. I could easily make those myself.

I turned my attention to the list. And these were the things I settled on.

Outfit
Black fedora.
Black mask.
Long, black, full-length leather overcoat.
Black trousers – jeans or leather.
Black top.
Black boots, possibly steel toe-capped.
Body armour!!! – black!!! – Knee/shin pads. Gloves (black leather). Stab-proof vest!!! (essential)

Vehicle
Black Ford Mustang!!!

<u>Name</u>
~~Justice Man~~
~~Vengeance Master~~
~~The People's Avenger~~
~~King Punish~~
The REVENGELIST!!!

* * *

I thought long and hard about the name. It had to sound good. In the end, I decided that The Revengelist had the best ring to it. I opened Photoshop, and tinkered with some ideas for my 'business card'.

The car might be the hardest thing to pull off, although not impossible. I couldn't see The Revengelist driving my battered-up Vauxhall Astra, so I had to try. Besides, I needed something that the police wouldn't be able to trace the minute I whizzed past them or got flashed by a speed camera. All these damn ANPR cameras would give me away in no time. I needed to avoid that paper trail. So false registration details. No insurance, no tax. No connection to me whatsoever. A Ford Mustang might stand out, of course. They weren't exactly inconspicuous, but fuck it. If I'd lived in a small town, it might have been a bigger problem but a city was basically just a big old mish-mash of freaks; easier to go unnoticed. And besides... it wasn't every day you decided to suit up and fight crime, so it didn't seem like too much to ask to be able to push the boat out a little.

Weapons were easy and improvisation would suffice on most jobs anyway.

My outfit... that could be assembled from orders with various online clothing retailers. A sex-shop for a leather mask, perhaps. A hat-shop for the fedora. The clothing was no problem. The armour, though; maybe a different story.

And then I figured I could make a stab-proof vest of my own from some sort of hunting-jacket, by inserting metal plates into the lining.

It could actually work!

* * *

I made up my mind on one other thing, too.

As much as I hated my job, it would prove to be a valuable resource. I would have given it up if there was anything to gain from doing that. But there wasn't. There was more to gain by staying there, slogging it out, soaking up intelligence.

I had everything I needed for targeting the rotten bastards right there in my office.

Six

Finding a sex-shop was no problem. I rang them on Monday morning from my desk, withholding my number. The office door shut, one hand over the mouthpiece. I had a clear idea in my mind of what I wanted, and had taken head measurements. Whispering into the phone, I outlined my wishes to the woman on the other end of the line.

I wanted a black leather face-mask, wide eye-holes, a zip up the back to secure the thing when I was wearing it. I asked her to create a mouth-hole with an upward-curving semi-circular shape. Metal pins vertically barring the opening. Think of Hannibal Lecter's mask in *The Silence of the Lambs*.

Something along those lines.

* * *

Also, from my office, I was able to buy the clothing I needed. Browsing multiple sites, I placed my orders and paid by card. One thing from *here*, another from over *there*. I didn't want to assemble my costume from just one retailer who might recognise the combination when worn by The Revengelist and therefore lead the police straight to my door.

I searched for a black Ford Mustang, too. Nothing too flashy. I didn't want to spend a damn fortune on it. The one I liked most was being sold privately, just over fifty miles out of town. I contacted the seller, got some information and told him I'd be there at 11am on Saturday to look it over. I left my name as Benjamin Brown.

During Friday's lunch-hour, I went to my bank and withdrew some cash which I stashed in my briefcase.

On Saturday morning, I was up early. Dressed casually, with fake specs and a fake moustache. I went by taxi. A large house, a flashy suburb. Huge drive and electric gates. I was greeted with a friendly handshake (which itched with grime straight away) and shown to the guy's garage. He was obviously a petrol-head. He spouted a bunch of facts about the Mustang I neither understood nor cared about. I only wanted it for the fact it looked so damn cool.

There were other vehicles there, all in various states of disrepair, and it looked like he bought them in, did them up and sold them on.

I spent a while looking around the Mustang, pretending I knew something about it. I looked under the bonnet and nodded approvingly without a clue about what I was nodding at. I sat in the driver's seat, fired up the engine and pumped the accelerator enthusiastically. I didn't make much conversation. Avoided eye-contact.

Eventually, the guy asked me whether I was interested. I told him I was. He was selling it for twelve thousand pounds and he said let's talk money, and I said I had ten grand in my briefcase, cash – take it or leave it. His eyes bulged greedily and he made an effort to push me further. I told him that I would walk away with my money right there and then. In the end, we shook on ten, went through to his kitchen and sat down at the breakfast table. I removed the bundles of cash from my briefcase and waited patiently as he counted them.

* * *

A while later, I was driving back home in my Mustang. I gave the guy a fake address and drove off. Easy as. Nothing would be traced to me. Disguise, fake name, fake address.

I stashed the car in my garage and removed the plates. Covered the car with a large tarpaulin, put the plates and paperwork in a box-file and took them inside the house.

* * *

Over the next few days, parcels started arriving in the post. I opened each one of them excitedly and admired the items within. I waited before trying anything on, though. It had to be done together. The outfit, when assembled in its entirety, had to be seen as one outfit. I cleared out a closet and placed the items into a black suitcase.

I printed off a bunch of my hand-made business cards, placed them into a card-holder. Getting all prepared.

Not long now, I thought.

* * *

My shin-pads and hunting-vest were the last items to come. By that time, I had several steel plates ready and waiting. I'd approached a secondary school headmaster and commissioned the metal-work department to make them for me in return for a substantial contribution to the school funds, which I knew were always crying out for substantial contributions.

When the vest arrived, I spent a few hours unpicking the stitching, inserting the steel plates, and stitching the seams back up. I checked it over and smiled a self-satisfied smile.

It was a damn good job, and one that should protect me from unfelt injuries.

* * *

It was one week after I'd picked up the Mustang. My mobile rang.

"Hello, Mr Brown," said the woman from the sex-shop. "Your mask is ready for collection."

* * *

I stood in front of a full-length mirror, fully kitted out. The Revengelist looked back, faceless and menacing.

The mask was excellent. I fucking *loved* it! With my black fedora tipped forward, a menacing shadow was cast across my eyes. I looked awesome. A cross between Blade and Rorschach from *Watchmen*.

I moved around, admiring the costume. Striking poses. Flexing the leather gloves and making punches in the air. It was so good I couldn't help but laugh to myself. And I got to thinking. In the new *Dark Knight* trilogy, Christian Bale had disguised his voice by lowering it to a growl. That was worth copying.

I practised for a while. Doing the whole "You talking to me?" thing like Robert De Niro in *Taxi Driver*. Psyching myself up.

Eventually, I was ready. And I wanted to break the outfit in.

* * *

I drew up a few rules which went something like this:

1. Guilt may be determined based upon a skilful assessment of evidence.
2. Punishment must be proportionate to the offence committed.
3. Death must not result where death is not proportionate.

During my last stint in the office, I'd compiled a list of targets. It contained the names, addresses and criminal activities of three clients.

The first on my list was Johnny Clayton, a prolific shoplifter. The second was Mick Miller, a photographer charged with raping a woman who was modelling nude for him. The third was Reginald Chesterfield.

I was keen to get started there and then, so I whittled down the choices. My gloved finger danced over the names as I went.

"Eeny, meany, miney, mo, catch a scumbag by the toe, even if he squeals don't let him go, eeny, meany, miney, mo!"

Mick was out.

I went again.

And Johnny was out. Which left Reginald Chesterfield.

Seven

Reginald lived alone in a nice part of town. He was retired, with a shitload of money tucked away. Cancer had killed his wife a few years back. To fill the hole left by her death, Reginald went for a job as Santa and by all accounts, he was good at it. He sure as hell *looked* like Santa. But in the privacy of his own home, he was getting his kicks looking at some of the worst examples of 'child porn' on the internet.

Research for a book, he'd said... But I didn't believe a word of it.

I gathered up my weapon for the night from the garage and slid it into my coat pocket. I whipped the tarpaulin off the Mustang, jumped in, backed it out of the garage and off my drive. Aimed it in the direction of Reginald's end of town and roared away.

Reginald's was a terraced three-floor town house. A light was on in a window on the first floor. Probably the lounge. This time, I wasn't so concerned with discretion. I got out the car, marched across the street and kicked his front door open. I heard the sound of urgent footsteps on the ceiling above me. Reginald had jumped from his seat and was running somewhere. I flew up the stairs to the next floor, two at a time. I heard the clumping of his feet on the upper flight. A door slammed. A lock clicked into place.

I was outside the bedroom door in a matter of seconds. I tried the handle, but it didn't budge.

"*GET OUT!*" Reginald's scream was terror-stricken.

I tapped lightly on the door. Lowered my voice. "Little pig? Let me in."

My adrenaline levels had my heart pumping. It was fun freaking him out like this. Like Jack Torrance in *The Shining*.

"*Leave me alone!*" His voice was hysterical. He'd fled the lounge so quickly he hadn't had time to grab a phone. He was trapped.

"No can do," I said, and I kicked his door. The lock smashed. Great splinters skewed off from the frame as the door flew open. Reginald jumped back with a shriek. There was a dark stain of piss at his crotch.

* * *

I burst into the room and aimed a punch at Reginald's face. He went down and didn't get up. I hoisted him up and laid him flat on the bed, belly up. I went to the bedroom closet, found some ties and took one. I went to work with the parcel tape. Stuffed the tie in his mouth and taped over it.

Then I stood at the foot of the bed waiting for him to wake.

Within minutes he was snuffling and groaning through the gag, squirming around, Just like Leon Hunt. Blood was trickling from his nose, into his white beard. He saw me, and his eyes bulged.

"You've been a *dirty* boy, Reginald."

Reginald tried to scream for help. But the muffled sound that came out would alert nobody. He was fucked, and he knew it. The desperation on his face, the inner torment. Eyes frantically searching for something. A phone, maybe; a route for escape.

"A disgusting pervert!" I said.

I removed the secateurs from my pocket. Unclipped the catch and held them up for Reginald to see. I squeezed them shut a couple of times, *snippety-snip*. And Reginald began crying. He rolled into the foetal position, presumably understanding where this was going. Tears and snot streaming down his face.

"Please," he sobbed. Coming through the gag it was all muffled, but I knew begging when I heard it.

I looked at him and felt nothing. Absolutely nothing. He was nothing but a fucking pervert.

I squeezed the secateurs together again.

"You kiddie-fiddling fuckers make me sick," I said. "And at first, I wasn't sure whether to stab your eyes out to stop you looking at this filth. But in the end, I think the choice was pretty obvious, really."

Reginald was shaking his head, eyes bulging with terror in a last-ditch effort to plead with me. Squirming and twisting and wriggling as the inevitability of it all became clearer.

I clambered on to the bed, sat astride his legs. Pinning him down. He writhed around, but it didn't matter. With one gloved hand, I unbuckled his belt, unzipped his fly and yanked his pissy underwear down. His exposed penis lay limp and shrivelled.

* * *

Reginald was screaming through the gag. The blood coming from the wound in his groin was unstoppable. Surging with the pulsing rhythm of his blood-flow, spilling over his hips and soaking into the bed sheets. Blood-puddles on the mattress.

I dipped one hand into my pocket and removed a card, placed it gently on the pillows.

Holding his amputated penis in one hand, I walked from the room, down the landing, down the stairs. I went to the phone in the hallway, picked up the receiver, dialled 999. I asked for an ambulance, gave Reginald's address.

"What's the emergency, please?" said the operator.

"I just cut a kiddie-fiddler's dick off," I said, and dropped the receiver back.

As I left, I threw Reginald's floppy dead penis into one of the bins out front. Exactly where it belonged.

Eight

VIGILANTE STRIKES!
"Justice is Served" Says Masked Avenger

Police are searching for a masked vigilante calling himself The Revengelist after an attack on retired Mr Reginald Chesterfield of Hampton Row.

Police want to speak to anyone who may have information after the assailant forced entry to Mr Chesterfield's home on the evening of Friday 5th October and savagely assaulted him with a pair of garden secateurs, before alerting the emergency services. Mr Chesterfield, 75, who works during the Christmas season as a department store Father Christmas, is currently on court bail facing numerous allegations of possessing indecent images of children. In light of the message left at the scene, police believe that this was a vigilante-style attack.

Detective Chief Insp Rodney Lucas had this to say:

"This was a horrific attack on an elderly man in his own home. The police want the public to know that vigilantism will not be tolerated. We are the enforcers of the law, and the actions of this individual are neither welcome nor acceptable."

At this stage, the police have no leads as to the identity of the vigilante, but warn that he may be armed and dangerous. Police also believe that this attack may be linked to an earlier attack on Mr Leon Hunt, of Cherry Tree Close.

Mr Hunt, twenty and unemployed, was released on bail following a charge of robbery and was attacked in his home the same evening, suffering a broken leg after being gagged and bound in parcel tape.

Police confirm that the vigilante's message "Justice is Served" was found at this earlier scene.

* * *

A busy fortnight, but one thing I hadn't forgotten was Rachel. I was a little worried that she might have thought I had, so I composed a text message.

– *Have been busy. But have not 4gotten u. I figure it is your turn 2 invite me to dinner?*
I hit send. Half an hour later she texted me back.

– *Nice to finally hear from u! I would luv to have dinner again, but I have plans all wk. How about next weekend?*
I responded immediately.

– *That's cool! Sat 7.30?*
Her reply:

– *The Lobster Pot in town – it's a thing!*

* * *

"TOOTH FAIRY" KILLS AGAIN
City in Fear as Serial Killer Claims New Victims

Police have widened their search for serial murderer dubbed "The Tooth Fairy" after what police describe as another horrific attack left two more dead. Information at this stage confirms that a house on Frindsbury Lane was broken into after parents John and Laura Kline left for the evening to attend a work function, leaving twenty-year-old baby-sitter Michelle Taylor in charge of their eight-year-old daughter Rhianna Kline.

The intruder, in what police say is becoming a grotesque trademark feature of the murders, restrained the victims before beating them to death. Each victim was found sitting on a one pound coin.

Tributes have been flooding in for the deceased girls as the local community is shaken. Local residents have been laying floral tributes, cards and candles. Many residents have spoken of their grief, describing the victims as "lovely girls". Police had only this to say:

"Be under no illusions. This monster will be caught and brought to justice."

* * *

I was back in the office, first thing Monday morning. Over a coffee in the kitchen, Harry sparked up conversation.

"You hear about that Tooth Fairy bastard?"

I nodded. "Yeah. Sick fucker."

"I'm getting fed up with this shit, Jack. I mean it. Making an income is important, but is it *more* important than defending these scumbag rapists, thieves and murderers? Playing a part in having these people put back on our streets? Would you be happy defending a man like that Tooth Fairy on the basis that it benefits you financially?"

"Not particularly," I said. "But someone has to."

That, at least, was true.

"Perhaps. But perhaps this Revengelist guy has got the right idea," he said thoughtfully.

"Justice is for the courts, surely? Taking the law into our own hands is dangerous."

Harry frowned. "It is," he said. "At least in principle, anyway. But how often do the courts get it right, Jack? How many times have we been mortified by a bad decision? How many times have you read a newspaper interview with a victim, or a victim's family, agreeing that the bastards who wronged them got what they truly deserved?"

He was right about that. I'd known it for a long time.

"What about the police?" I said.

"Forget the police," said Harry. "They're no better. I give them credit for trying, but they're under-funded, under-staffed and over-zealous. If you ask me, this guy, The Revengelist, may be doing the whole damn system a favour."

"Really?"

"Of course!" he said. "Look at Reginald Chesterfield. Sick bastard! What do you think people were thinking he *really* deserved? Not probation. Not rehabilitation. He deserved *exactly* what that guy did to him, that's what."

"Hmm," I said.

"The justice system's in a mess," he went on. "Has been for a long time. The CPS is stretched to breaking point, and being stretched even further all the time. Victims, and potential future victims, are not being made to feel protected nor given the peace of mind that true justice has been done."

I paused for a moment, my belly fluttering with excitement. Knowing that Harry was pretty much justifying my actions, without realising The Revengelist was sat right in front of him... it was really quite exhilarating.

"Heavy fucking stuff, man," I said.

Nine

Mick Miller was next on my list. I didn't have any ideas for dealing with Johnny Clayton. I could have gone and chopped his hands off, but after Reginald Chesterfield I felt it lacked imagination.

With Miller, though, I knew.

I decided to suit up. And I wasn't going to need a blade. Instead, I went to the fridge and got just what I *did* need.

Then I headed for the Mustang.

* * *

Mick Miller lived on the first floor of a house split into two flats. He was a forty-nine-year-old photographer with his own little studio up in his flat and he regularly paid women to strip for his pictures. He said that he liked to explore the fragility and sensitivity of nudity. The privacy. To turn it from a social taboo into a reflection of its beauty. He took pictures of naked women in poses of caught-in-the-act nakedness. He liked to convey expressions of shame, embarrassment and surprise in caricatured exaggeration. In this respect, he said, he was forcing the audience to confront its feelings.

I just thought it was a bad excuse for being a fucking pervert.

He was facing an allegation of rape. The victim was a twenty-four-year-old model. She claimed that during a photo-shoot, Miller was instructing her to strike increasingly erotic positions, which she began to feel more and more uncomfortable with. The final straw was when he asked her to simulate being caught masturbating. She refused, and he got angry. As she started to dress, he got violent and he raped her.

Miller agreed that he had requested the masturbation pose, but said that she'd actually complied. He'd never taken the pictures, though. He said the atmosphere was intensely sexual and there was already an obvious attraction between the two of them. They went on to have sex instead, and she told him several times to 'make it rough.'

Afterwards, the woman sobbed and told him that she shouldn't have slept with him. She had a boyfriend who would hurt her when he found out what she had done. So, she dressed, and left his flat in a hurry.

Miller suggested, when asked by the police what reason the victim might have for fabricating the allegation, that she was obviously in fear of a beating from her boyfriend and it was easier for her to deny infidelity by claiming rape. I had never believed it. It was too convenient an explanation to account for her injuries. The bite marks on her buttocks and breasts. And I had nothing against people who fulfilled their sexual pleasures by sadomasochistic exploration. All the fuss about E. L. James's *Fifty Shades* books and the so-called disempowerment of women was a short-cut to thinking. Book-burning organisers were no better than the Nazis, reducing freedom of expression to a freedom that exists only if it suits the masses.

But I didn't buy it.

His account was challenged by the victim's boyfriend, who confirmed that in their whole six-year relationship, rough sex wasn't something they were into. They had neither tried it nor ever been interested in it. In my opinion, this reduced the credibility of Miller's account.

I parked the Mustang just around the corner, and walked back to the flat. There were two intercom buzzers by the front door. But looking at them made me realise I didn't have a convincing excuse for him to release the door.

It was dark. Unless he was expecting someone to just suddenly turn up, he may not answer the buzzer, let alone open the door to a complete stranger with word on the street of a vigilante prowling around.

I decided to investigate further. I found that at the end of the row of houses was an alleyway which led round the back gardens. Making a mental note of Miller's house number, I walked up the alley and took a left to the gardens. I counted off the houses, and found myself facing a wooden fence. There was a large gate, and I tried the handle. It opened.

I went into the garden.

* * *

Hiding behind a large bush, I could see that Miller's kitchen window was lit. The light spilled down into the garden, illuminating a scruffy lawn that no one seemed to have bothered tending. Miller wouldn't have been able to see me, even if I had stood in the centre of the garden waving at him. The light inside would have turned his kitchen window into a mirror against the darkness outside. I could now see that he was pottering around in the kitchen, preparing a microwave meal.

I stood watching for about ten minutes. Then he disappeared, and out went the kitchen light.

This was it.

I climbed up the drainpipe. An old metal one; a little rusty in places, but it held. I climbed up and then stepped on to the window ledge, holding on to the guttering. Both feet were on the ledge, my hands had a good grip. With a strong kick, the window shattered and I jumped into the kitchen.

* * *

Miller was suddenly in the doorway. His backlit features an ugly mask of terror. He had no trousers on. Just a T-shirt and underpants.

"What the fuck?" he muttered.

"It's punishing time!" I said, leaping forwards.

Miller turned to sprint for his front door, which was on the landing at the top of the stairs. But I moved much quicker than he did and grabbed him from behind with one gloved hand covering his mouth. I grabbed his left arm and wrestled it into a half-nelson. He winced in pain, but was powerless. I manoeuvred him back down the hall to his front room.

"Down," I said. "Face down!"

I carefully guided him down to his knees without releasing the grip on his arm or the hand over his mouth. He went down and then lay flat on his belly, whimpering as he went. I sat on his back, pinning him down, and let go of his arm. I took out the parcel tape from my coat pocket, let go of his mouth and quickly sealed it shut with several layers of the tape. He struggled. I told him not to but he didn't listen. I took his wrists and bound them tightly behind his back and within minutes he was another squirming maggot.

I stood, and smoothed out my coat. Adjusted my hat. Just like everyone else, he was a mess. I looked at him, repulsed.

"You're a sick rapist," I said. "Did you think you'd get away with it?"

He squealed, and shook his head frantically.

I looked around his flat. Over in the bay-window, his studio. A raised platform with a white backdrop. Professional lighting rigs. A large and expensive-looking camera positioned several feet back. One of those silvery umbrella things. Near me was a computer, and on it, Windows Media Player was up. It was playing a movie. Next to the monitor was a box of tissues.

"Did I catch you at a bad time?"

Miller started crying. And then I clocked the images on the monitor.

As I remember it, the police had requested authority for an s.18 search following his arrest. As his lawyer, I had objected. The investigating officer had pleaded with the inspector that because of his profession, photographic evidence of the rape may exist. I pointed out that there were no reasonable grounds to suspect this. I pointed out that even the victim had stated that the alleged rape had occurred well away from the camera, which was always pointing at the 'stage' area. And that there were certainly no indicators in the victim's account that Miller had documented the alleged rape. The inspector had agreed with me and declined to authorise a search.

But I should have kept my mouth shut. The images on the screen were very clear indeed.

I turned away in disgust.

"So," I said. "You secretly *filmed* it!"

Miller was shrieking.

* * *

I found a spool of blank DVDs. I copied the wretched film over, burnt it, and ejected the newly made disk. I found an envelope, slipped it inside, and wrote on the envelope in marker pen.

For The Police.

Then I took out a business card and taped it to the envelope.

From the inside pocket of my coat, I removed the object I had taken from my fridge. It was a large cucumber.

I kneeled down and yanked off Miller's underpants.

"This is going to hurt," I said. "But I *know* you like it rough!"

I rammed the cucumber up his arse so hard something inside him ripped. His choked screams were full of torment, and even I winced as he passed out.

It would take a doctor to get that thing back out.

* * *

From Miller's phone, I dialled 999. I asked for the police. I gave the operator his name and address.

"You may want to bring an ambulance," I said. "He's in a bad way."

I hung up the phone, and picked up the envelope. I taped it to Miller's back and left his flat the front way.

* * *

POLICE BAFFLED

New Evidence Emerges in Rape Case after Vigilante Strikes for Third Time

Vigilante "The Revengelist" struck once more, leaving police baffled as Mr Michael Miller, forty-nine, of Gordon Road, who is on court bail for charges of rape, was viciously assaulted in his flat on Monday night after being gagged and bound in parcel tape. Police have confirmed that "incriminating evidence" relating to Mr Miller's court case was discovered at the scene which a source close to the police inform us may seriously affect the viability of Mr Miller's defence. Mr Miller was rushed to hospital for emergency treatment after a cucumber was forcefully inserted into his anus. Police are still appealing to the public for information that might lead to an arrest of the vigilante. However, supporters of The Revengelist are very keen to remind the police that without the vigilante's intervention, this vital new piece of evidence would never have been discovered.

* * *

Saturday. I was showered, shaved and dressed by quarter to seven. I booked a cab to take me to the Lobster Pot in town. It turned up at ten past, and I was standing outside the Pot at twenty-five past. The late-autumn sky was dark. The stars clear and bright. There was a chill in the air, but it was fresh.

At twenty-five to eight, a cab pulled up. With a genuine smile, Rachel slid from the back seat, paid the driver and walked up to me. All the excitement and attraction from our last date came flooding back, and I was glad to see her again. I regretted that it had taken me two weeks to contact her, but then again, I felt that it might look a bit too eager if I had.

"Hello, Mr Jones," she said, smiling.

"Hello, officer." I gestured for her to lead, ladies first. She went into the restaurant and I followed.

* * *

Rachel ordered steak. I went for a burger and we shared a house red.

"I thought you might ring me sooner," said Rachel, feigning hurt feelings.

"I might have done," I said, "had it not been for work commitments. I've really been under a lot of pressure recently."

"I suppose I was just worried that I might have frightened you off. A woman's ego is a fragile thing, Mr Jones."

I sipped my wine and then smiled at her. Her comment had revealed more than I thought she'd meant to give away, and that was nice.

"Officer," I said. "I have thought of little else *but* ringing you. I thoroughly enjoyed my evening with you, and was keen to see you again."

Okay, so I'd been busy and there'd been a lot on my mind. But it wasn't a total lie. I really liked her.

Rachel smiled. "Talk about desperate!" she said.

I laughed and realised that I hadn't laughed properly in two weeks.

Our food came, and as we ate, we chatted. That flirty vibe was there again. We ordered more wine and after the meal, we chose dessert. We went for chocolate fudge cake. When our plates had been collected, I picked up the bill, following a bit of protest from Rachel on the matter. And it was about a quarter to ten by the time we were gathering up our coats. We stepped out onto the street.

"I would invite you back," said Rachel, "but I recorded a documentary I want to catch up with. I hope you don't mind."

I smiled politely. "Not at all."

She whacked my arm, laughing. "I was joking," she said. "Come on, we'll get a cab."

We walked to a taxi-rank and Rachel linked her arm through mine, pressing up tightly against me in the autumn chill.

* * *

I woke the next day with Rachel snuggled up to me.

It had been a while since I'd last slept with a woman. Rachel was twenty-six like me, and had been in one long-term relationship which had ended in disaster two nights before her wedding. She seemed reluctant to go into too much detail about that. And I was comfortable enough with it. I'd had a few girlfriends, but nothing meaningful enough to even compare to the feeling I had being with Rachel.

I carefully lifted her arm from off my chest and started to rise. As I did, Rachel roused.

"Where do you think you're going?" she said.

"I've got to go. There's a few things I need to do."

"What could be more compelling than lying here with me?" she said. We both smiled.

I leaned in towards her for a kiss, and she said:

"One for the road, Mr Jones?"

Ten

When I got home, I started thinking about this Tooth Fairy bastard. He needed stopping. Maybe I was the person to do that. But as I knew only too well, I had limited means for investigating. There *was* Rachel. I could try to get information from her, but I didn't want to use her, nor risk exposing who I was. I genuinely liked her. I sensed that she was a woman I could truly fall in love with. I didn't want her to think I was some sort of nut-job or put her in a difficult position. As an officer of the law, she would have a very straightforward obligation to shop me. But as I suspected that she had feelings for me too, it would present her with a moral dilemma, and I desperately wanted to avoid her having to choose between me and her integrity.

In a society full of incompetence, apathy and corruption, good honest coppers were essential. Rachel's integrity had to be maintained, *at all costs*. She must never find out who I was.

So, I ruled out Rachel as a means of catching The Tooth Fairy.

This left me very few options. I could put word out on the street – a reward for information leading to his capture. With growing support for The Revengelist, it could work.

But what about the police? They clearly had the means to put out a bigger and more substantial reward, and their investigation would be underway already.

Me? I was still just tinkering with ideas.

I considered brainstorming with my current information about him and seeing what I could come up with. But the problem with that was all that I knew about him was what the media had reported, and I therefore knew just the same as everyone else. I had no particular advantage there.

The only thing I had going for me was that the police had procedures and rules, and had to comply with them. I on the other hand, did not.

But I was still stumped. It seemed there *was* no way I could hunt The Tooth Fairy. Not without more information. Not without breaking some rules. Because when he eventually did make a mistake and get caught, I wouldn't be able to get justice. He'd immediately be remanded into custody. There'd be no way that mad fucker would get bail.

And then it struck me.

* * *

Giles Rickman was a spoilt rich kid with a taste for large amounts of marijuana and a knowledge of computer hacking that was probably sufficient to bring NASA out in cold sweats.

His father was a rich toff with a large country house he opened to the viewing public in summer. Giles had lived a good life. But he'd grown tired of the whole façade of money, horses, and pretentious tweed-wearing sycophants. He'd hooked up with some dope-smoking, poetry-reading beatniks and built the plans for an underground operation to hack the major banks' computer systems in order to refund massive interest rates on loans back to the customers.

He was the founder of an army of so-called cyber-terrorists, trying to administer Robin Hood-style wealth redistribution. He called it 'The League of Equalisers.' Someone in his circle had been a police informer, but before the police had been able to seize his plans, he'd successfully hidden it all. Although to him it was several years' worth of research and planning down the drain, it had been the thing that spared him a long spell in prison.

And we'd represented him.

* * *

I drove to the office in my civvies. It wasn't the first time I'd been in the office on a weekend, and Robert knew I sometimes did it. Our file on Giles would have been up in the attic space, in storage. I just had to boot up the computer system and trace the file number. All files in storage were recorded, so once I knew its number, it was little more than going upstairs, and pulling out the file.

About half an hour later, I was driving away from the office with Giles Rickman's last known address.

* * *

It was 3am and I was sitting in the Mustang outside Giles's address, suited up. It was a small two-bedroom house. I recalled that he worked nights in a supermarket, and wouldn't be home until about 6am.

I sat and watched the house for a while, debating with myself whether to risk breaking in. In the end, I decided I would. I needed to speak to him, and would wait until he got home.

* * *

I heard keys jingling in his front door at about ten to six. I was sitting in an armchair in his front room. He shut the door behind him and came into the lounge.

Even in the early morning gloom, he saw the shape of me sitting in his chair. "Sit down," I said.

He didn't move. "What do *you* want?"

"I need your help. Sit down."

Giles stepped into the room cautiously. He dropped his coat and bag on the sofa, and sat down.

"Are you going to hurt me?"

"No," I said. "That's a promise."

Giles didn't look convinced. "How can I—"

"Trust me? Because if I *wanted* to hurt you, we wouldn't be having this conversation."

To a degree, this seemed to satisfy him. I sensed him relax slightly.

"What *do* you want?"

I leaned forward in the armchair and my leathers creaked in the silence.

"I want to engage your services."

Giles looked at me. His expression gave little away, but there *was* a slight flicker of relief.

"I don't do that anymore," he said.

I laughed politely. "Mr Rickman," I said. "I assume you have read about me in the papers?"

"I may have read something," he said.

"Then you will know what I do. Have you heard of The Tooth Fairy?"

He nodded. "Yes."

"Good," I said. "He needs stopping, Mr Rickman. And with your help, that is something I intend to do. Understand?"

"I do," he said.

I nodded. "I thought you would. So help me."

* * *

The flicker of relief now appeared to be more of a spark of intrigue. I'd aroused his curiosity. Not his commitment; not yet. But certainly his interest.

"What do you want me to do?"

"I can't even begin to look for him without a lead," I said. "I need to know what the police know."

Giles was silent for a moment. Thinking it through. But there was a grim look on his face.

"You'd be generously rewarded," I said.

"How much?"

"Two now, and two later."

Again, Giles went off into his own thoughts.

"How would the information benefit *you*?"

It was a good question with a very valid point but it was none of his fucking business.

"Let me worry about that," I said.

"What makes you think I won't take the money now and vanish? Or maybe shop you to the police?"

I nodded, smiling. "You could," I said. "But I'm confident you won't. You *know* the things I do, after all."

Giles didn't answer. I hadn't wanted to make any kind of threat. Not really. I needed this guy to help me, for Christ's sake.

"Look," I said. "I have no doubt that some people think I'm a dangerous mad man. But there *are* those who see that I am not just hurting people randomly. Look at that filthy rapist. Without me, the police wouldn't have the tape he made. I'm doing a good thing, Giles. In fact, we even sing from similar hymn-books. Can you see that?"

Giles nodded. "I can," he said. And he sounded genuine.

"Are you in?"

"You won't come for me afterwards?"

I stuck out my gloved hand. "I give you my word."

Giles shook it and then I stood. "I'll be back in one week."

I removed two thousand pounds from an inside pocket, threw the bundle into his lap and left.

Eleven

I'd never known Harry's age until the day Robert told me about the heart attack.

I'd just assumed he was in his late forties, but I was wrong. He was actually in his early fifties, although his age had *nothing* to do with the heart attack.

Harry had been at home with his wife Clarissa and teenage daughter, Mandy. They'd all settled down for the night when an intruder woke them. Bleary-eyed, Harry ushered Mandy into his room with Clarissa, intending to keep them both safe. With a baseball bat he kept in his room, he crept downstairs. But the intruder took him by surprise, wrestled the baseball bat from him and bashed him over the head with it. Whilst Harry was unconscious, the intruder went upstairs, groped fifteen-year-old Mandy and made off with almost every valuable item of jewellery they possessed.

When Harry came to, he found his wife cradling Mandy in the bedroom. His daughter was in a state of shock – her face vacant and lost to some deep and private sanctuary.

He suffered a heart attack right there on the spot.

* * *

The police acted quickly.

They caught the piece of shit and hauled him in. He asked for a defence lawyer from Bond, Jenkins & Coleridge, one of those crooked law firms I hated. A real bunch of slimy bastards. The solicitor was a guy called Rupert Bond and by all accounts, the local criminals knew him as The Devil's Advocate. It was no surprise that the rotten little fucker had asked for him.

What *was* a surprise, when I heard it, was that the scumbag was one of my own clients. One of my regulars.

Johnny Clayton.

* * *

Following his interview, Clayton was bailed for further investigations. He'd put forward an alibi. Something Bond had probably helped him cook up.

As far as Harry was concerned, he'd never seen the intruder, and could neither confirm nor deny that the person had been Clayton. Clarissa and Mandy on the other hand, gave descriptions.

* * *

Harry was hooked to a drip and various machines that monitored his well-being. I sat down by his bed, put the grapes I'd bought for him on his bedside table. He didn't look so good, but I suspected he looked better than he had a couple of nights before. Clarissa had disappeared to allow me the private word I'd requested.

"Jack," he said. He sounded pleased to see me, yet there was a sense of confusion.

"Hi Harry," I said. "How are you?"

"Well, you know. Been better."

"Yeah, Robert filled me in."

"He did?" Harry sounded surprised.

"Yeah." I wasn't sure how to tackle the subject I wanted to raise. There was a momentary silence between us.

"They got someone," I said. "I didn't know whether you knew that."

"Yeah?"

"He's been bailed for further enquiries."

Harry was just looking at me. He really didn't look so good.

"Harry," I said. "I'm so sorry that this happened to you. To your family."

There was a tear rolling down Harry's cheek. "Mandy," he said.

It was all he could say.

I reached out, took hold of Harry's hand. He looked at me, and I fixed his eyes with a look of honest sincerity.

"Justice will be served, Harry."

His watery eyes suddenly changed. In that look, I saw awareness firm up. A sudden *knowing*.

"You?"

I looked at him for a long time. Said nothing. But he knew.

I released his hand. "Clarissa will be back any minute," I said. "I've got to go now, Harry. Okay?"

Harry nodded. "Take care," he said.

As I walked around his bed, I turned to look at him one last time.

"He'll pay," I told him.

And then I left.

* * *

Johnny Clayton was a prolific shoplifter. That much, I knew. He'd also dabbled with some burglary. Touching up a fifteen-year-old kid was out of character. But if there was one thing I had learned over the years; it was not to be surprised by the capabilities of all the rotten bastards in this world.

Still, I felt bad. It hadn't been so long ago that I'd put Clayton to the back of my list. I thought my ideas for dealing with him 'lacked imagination.'

I should have gone for him earlier. I should have cut his fingers off and fed them to him. I should have done something. The decision not to had been a bad one. Harry's family had suffered because of it. Because of me. It was *my* fault. So tonight, Clayton was going to get hurt.

* * *

For the third time, I was dealing with a rotten fucking pervert.

Sitting in the Mustang, now parked outside Clayton's council house, I caressed the item I'd brought with me, and then stuffed them into my rucksack.

* * *

His front door burst open with the force of my heavy kick. Instantly, I was in the hall, then the lounge. Clayton was sprawled out on a sofa. Beside him was a used needle and some heroin paraphernalia. He was off his face. I stepped over to him, grabbed his jumper by the scruff and hoisted him up.

"Get up, you cunt!"

He mumbled something incoherent, and smiled. His eyes barely opened, a glazed and vacant look. He was far away somewhere, in a place only drug-users found comfort.

I slapped his face. Once, twice, three times.

"I'm talking to you, you piece of shit. Wake up!"

He seemed to register me.

"*Whothefuckareyou?*" he slurred.

"Who the fuck do I look like?"

His eyes focused on my mask. Sobriety began setting in. "Oh shit," he said.

"That's right," I said. "Now wake up. We got business."

* * *

Clayton was bleeding from his nose. I'd tied him to a chair from the kitchen and beaten him a bit. His face was pretty busted up now.

"I'm going to enjoy this more than I ought to," I told him.

"Fuck you!" he screamed at me.

I looked at him and said nothing. Seconds ticking by, stringing out the tension.

He screamed again. "*Fuck you!*"

I nodded. Went out to the kitchen, rummaged through the drawers and found a pair of scissors.

"You've got a filthy mouth, Johnny Boy!" I said, returning to the lounge.

Clayton sat still and looked at me. All his cockiness drained away. I stepped forward, grabbed his face with one hand and yanked his tongue out with the other. Releasing his cheeks, I held the tongue tightly and used the scissors to cut it out of his mouth. It wasn't as easy as I thought it might be. Aside from his struggling, there was a curious and fascinating similarity to the feeling of cutting through gristly steak, but in the end it came out and I stepped back, holding it between thumb and forefinger. Feeling it jiggle like a piece of jellied eel. Blood spurted down his chin and soaked into his jumper. The drugs must have helped numb the pain, but I reckon I'd knocked him down a peg or two. He looked like he'd gone a few rounds with Mike Tyson.

I threw the tongue at him and he squirmed with revulsion as it splatted against his cheek.

"From shoplifting to burglary to kiddie-fiddling. You've made some poor choices in life, Johnny, and I'm getting sick of you fucking perverts."

Clayton spat a thick wad of bloody phlegm at my boots and smiled defiantly with blood-stained teeth.

"You probably thought you'd get away with it," I said. "And that fucker Bond is as big an idiot as you, so I'm pleased to disappoint."

I stepped forward and took his left hand in mine. Bent down, looked him in the eye.

"Let's crack on with this," I said.

At that, I started to bend his fingers back, one by one. Snapping them like pencils, each with a loud *crack*; twisting them out of shape so that they stuck up at strange and unnatural angles. His hand looked like a mangled dinner fork after Uri Geller had been to work on it. His screams were gargles. Blood had collected at the back of his throat making him sound like Gollum in the throes of mental anguish.

I went to work on his right hand. Taking as much time over it as I could, but finding that it was over quicker than I expected.

But still, I hadn't finished with him yet.

"Here comes the *really* fun bit," I said.

* * *

I fired up the blowtorch I'd brought with me and thought about all the wonderful parts of his body that could be cooked whilst still attached to him. Clayton's drug-addled semi-consciousness had returned and he was now sagging in the chair. His head lolling around. His eyeballs rolled slowly up and blinked lazily a few times before he realised what I was holding. He began struggling against the restraints but his impaired motor skills lacked any strength.

But then suddenly my mobile rang. I felt it vibrating in my trouser pocket. With Clayton barely clinging to conscious, I decided to answer it.

"Jack?" It was Robert. He sounded depressed. Not his usual self at all.

"Yeah, it's me," I said.

"I have some bad news, I'm afraid."

"What is it?"

"Harry had another heart attack this evening. He didn't survive, Jack. Harry's dead."

I didn't know what the hell to say.

* * *

Clayton was now a murderer.

Robert filled me in. Harry had been hiding a heart condition for some time, even from his own wife. Shock had caused the first heart attack. But a few hours after my visit, Harry had suffered another and it killed him instantly. You take your victims as you find them, and if they've got underlying medical conditions, that's tough shit on you... but the question was, could evidential continuity from Clayton's assault and the subsequent heart attacks hold up in court?

It was possible, but I wasn't sure. Probably not for a murder charge. It was more likely a manslaughter charge, if anything. Not that it really mattered, anyway. I knew he was guilty, and that was enough.

I looked at Clayton. Christ, he was a mess. If only I had come after him first, as I should have done. None of this would have happened. He would have been too fucked up to mess with Harry's family.

But what now? I was feeling ill just looking at that rotten fucker and I wanted out.

My gaze fell upon the empty needle on the floor.

* * *

Death could not result from a punishment where death was not proportionate to the offence committed. That was one of my rules. But Harry was dead, and it was this bastard's fault.

But just as I thought this, I heard footsteps in the hall which then entered the lounge. And then a voice.

"*What the fuck!*"

I turned.

Standing in the doorway was Johnny Clayton's older brother, Bradley.

* * *

Bradley was a bigger, bulkier man than Johnny. In the blink of an eye, he was dashing across the room towards me. I lunged to one side, but he managed to grab me anyway. He rugby-tackled me to the ground and I landed with a painless thump. But thanks to my quick movement, he lost the advantage. I scrambled to my feet before he did, and when he got up he backed away from me towards the doorway again. Blocking my exit. Then he pushed the door shut. Propped in the corner was a well-worn baseball bat. I reckon it had probably smashed a few heads in its time. And without a doubt, my head would be next if I didn't act fast.

Bradley snatched it up double-quick, gripping it with both hands, poised like a batsman waiting for the pitch.

I side-stepped around Johnny's unconscious lump, backing up towards the sofa, not entirely sure where I was going with this. Bradley stepped towards me, eyes wide and unblinking. I watched him for a moment, then glanced around the room; options flitting through my head like sparrows in twilight.

Then I quickly bent down and grabbed up Johnny's needle. Retracted the plunger and sucked several millilitres of air into the chamber.

Bradley stepped closer. "I'm gonna smash your fucking skull in!"

I believed him. I moved closer to Johnny, approaching him from behind and keeping him between myself and Bradley.

"Step back," he said. "You stay away from him!"

I pressed the needle-point to a pulsing vein in Johnny's neck. The point sank easily through the skin, drawing a bead of blood. Bradley's eyes looked at me with the raw hatred of Hell-sent evil.

"I swear to God I'm going to kill you," he said. "Get away from him, now."

"Not just yet," I said.

And then I pushed the plunger.

* * *

As Johnny's body convulsed, Bradley lurched forward.

I'd seen a large glass paperweight on the mantelpiece behind me. I turned, picked it up and threw it as hard as I could at the lounge window. The window shattered.

Bradley's eyes were murderous hate. His brother was dead and he knew it. He looked from Johnny to me and moved suddenly in my direction.

I ran at the lounge window. Jumped, and crashed through it feeling nothing, broken glass spraying out onto the patch of grass out front. Then I dashed for the Mustang.

Bradley was sprinting from the front door.

I jumped into the car, started the engine and roared off. I looked in the rear-view, and saw Bradley hurl the bat after me. He was screaming into the chill autumn night.

Twelve

It was 5.30am, and one week exactly after my visit to Giles Rickman.

I waited for him to come home from work, sitting in the Mustang. It was a foggy morning, and the street-lights made misty orange pools of light. About ten to six, I saw Giles trudging down the pavement through the fog. He was carrying a Tesco's carrier bag with a flask in it.

As he stepped up to his front door, keys in hand, I said: "Hey."

He turned and looked at me. Nodded.

"Give me a moment," he said.

He disappeared in through the front door, and I wondered for a second whether he was ringing 999. I briefly considered driving away, worried that the flashing blue lights would arrive. But no. He was back out on the street again within a minute, and he looked both ways down the road before crossing to my car.

I had the driver's window down, and he crouched to look in.

"Everything I could get is on this," he said, holding up a USB memory stick.

"I'm very grateful," I said, taking it from him and stashing it in my coat pocket. I took a bundle of notes from my other pocket and gave it to him. "There's a little extra there," I said. "Consider it a tip."

Giles pocketed the cash. "Will I see you again?" he asked.

I looked at him.

"Not if you're a good boy," I said, then put the car into gear and drove off.

* * *

I put the USB stick into my computer. At first, my paranoia was telling me that Giles may have planted some horrible virus on it. I was reluctant to open its only folder. But I pushed the heebie-jeebies to one side. I double-clicked on the document folder and examined what it contained.

There was a sequence of digital crime-scene photos, but I had neither the desire nor the need to look at *them* right now. If push came to shove, I'd come back to them.

There were several CAD reports; contemporaneous records of incoming and outgoing phone calls. The dispatch of officers and initial observations. Everything date and time stamped.

Finally, there was a memo from some forensic psychologist called Raymond Hartley addressed to DCI Rodney Lucas. An informal profile assessment, by the looks of it.

I opened the memo and browsed its contents.

Hartley was asserting the opinion that The Tooth Fairy was clearly insane and possessed a terrible hatred of children. The act of twisting the fabled tooth fairy's actions was intended to frighten them, he said. The ones most receptive to its ability to terrorise the mind. From that act alone, The Tooth Fairy would have derived a great pleasure.

There was a possibility, he said, that this was someone who not only didn't like children but who came into contact with them often, probably through work. Contact that perpetuated and justified the hatred. It was probably someone intelligent, and someone who knew children well enough to know the things that would scare them. It was also likely to be someone who knew things about the families. Information that provided valuable assistance to the commission of the murders. Perhaps someone in a position of trust.

And on reading that, I closed the memo and smiled.

This was exactly the kind of information I'd needed.

* * *

In one of those 'Eureka' moments, I formed a theory of my own. With talk of psychopaths and child-hating, toothless corpses and positions of trust, I reckon I was bound to.

But was it just a crazy hunch born from hatred? Could it really be *him*?

* * *

I had to find some way of being sure.

Frank may well have been a complete bastard, but did I really think he was a murderer?

His relationship to me was by marriage only. I hated my Mum, and I felt no loyalty to either of them. He'd tried to systematically destroy me from the outside in. Being incapable of hurting me, he'd tried instead to rip my psyche apart.

But Frank? Respectable dentist? Upstanding member of society? Resentful of kids because he couldn't make his own?

Possibly.

Child-beating bastard?

Definitely.

Serial killer?

I didn't know, but I had to find out.

* * *

It was Monday morning. But Robert had closed the office for a few days as a mark of respect to Harry.

I slept most the way through. I woke around about 4.30pm, made myself a cheese-and-Marmite toasted sandwich. A strong coffee. I sat and made my plans.

* * *

His dental office was in town. I remember once being with him as a kid. He'd taken me to the office to sit quietly whilst he caught up with paperwork one weekend, and Mum had gone off shopping. I'd been half-listening to another dismal lecture from Frank about getting good grades in school, paying more attention to the code he punched into the alarm system. I had never forgotten it. I hoped like hell it hadn't changed.

It was late and it was dark but I had a torch. I forced his office door open. The alarm system bleeped its countdown. I went to the control panel and punched in the code. The countdown stopped.

I was in.

I went to the room I knew he kept his filing cabinet in, an office just slightly larger than a broom closet, and found his patient records. The drawers were alphabetised. I looked first for the Klines. And they were there. John, Laura and daughter Rhianna. I searched next for Michelle Taylor, and she, along with her family members, was there.

Lastly, I searched for the Wendles. Lance, Janice and son Jeff. They too, were there.

And now I had a lead. All The Tooth Fairy's victims were patients of Frank's.

If it was true that Frank, my step-father, was The Tooth Fairy, he was obviously using his patient list. Targeting his victims from the filing cabinet, in much the same way I had punished my clients. The sick *bastard*.

The thing to do now was find evidence that linked Frank to the murders.

* * *

Mum and Frank lived in a large house in the rural outskirts of town, paid for in part by Frank's job, and in part by Mum's divorce settlement. They had a monster of a dog; a huge German shepherd called Brutus, and Brutus had a free run of the ground-floor level.

The upper levels of the house were barred by a stair-gate and alarmed. After my success with the code for the offices, I knew I stood no chance here. Frank would never have let me see the code here. He would never have had a reason to. But it might not have mattered.

His study was downstairs.

And that just left Brutus.

* * *

Halloween. Mum and Frank *hated* Halloween. They hated the thought of kids begging for sweets and money at the best of times, but considered Halloween a night of glorified leeching and over-indulgence. They'd be in town, dining out to avoid the trick-or-treaters. It's what the always did.

In the days between breaking into Frank's office and now, I'd been to my doctor complaining of insomnia. He'd prescribed some sleeping-pills, but they weren't going to be for me.

Ten tablets in all. I stuffed each one of them into an individual raw sausage. The sausages into a plastic bag.

And as night fell, I suited up.

* * *

I parked the Mustang a few yards from the front drive of Mum and Frank's house. I got out and walked back. Just winging this. Not entirely sure how the whole thing would pan out.

I stood looking up the double-entry driveway, thinking carefully.

Then I stepped forwards. Creeping along, close to the dark bushes on the edges of the front drive. Using the shadows to hide me from any passers-by.

And the house loomed ahead of me. A vault of bad memories. Anguish. My weekend visits turning into the most dreadful times of my life. The bushes were the same ones that Frank told me vampire bats lived in. I was eight then, and I believed him. Just as I believed him when he told me the house was haunted by the ghost of a dead butler who hung himself in my bedroom.

The house seemed alive with the echoes of emotional torment. Of private misery and secret crying.

I stopped. Shook the memories away.

Get a fucking grip, I thought.

I removed the bag of sausages from my pocket and moved closer to the front door. Stepped up to it. Reached out a finger and pressed the doorbell, braced for seeing Frank's hateful eyes as the door opened.

But no. All that happened was that Brutus went mental. I heard him charging through the house, barking his stupidly loud bark and jumping at the door from the other side. He was freaking out; scratching and snuffling at the letter box.

Did he recognise me? Was he trained to sniff me out? Did he hate me just as much as Mum and Frank did?

Come on! I thought. *It's just a fucking dog.*

I quickly took out the sausages and posted them through the letter box. Brutus tried to bite my fingers as I poked the meat through but I felt no pain. Just a tugging feeling.

When I finished, I looked at my gloved hand. The leather was a little ripped, but the dog's teeth had not broken my skin. I looked at the letter box and whispered, "Sweet dreams, motherfucker."

I waited. Listening to the snaffling sounds. Brutus wolfing down the sausages.

I waited a while longer. Reached out and pressed the doorbell again.

This time, nothing.

*   *   *

The house was empty. Brutus was at the foot of the stairs, curled up against the stair-gate. Looking at him, I wasn't sure whether he was asleep or dead. Had I given him too much?

It's too fucking late now, I thought.

I moved down the hallway, counting off the doors. The study was at the end. Four doors down. Mum and Frank had redecorated since I last stepped foot through the front door. New carpets and a fresh lick of paint. My mind acknowledged the layout, but little else. I felt relieved; to see the house the way I remembered it might have freaked me out. A sense of confidence came back to me.

And then I was standing outside the study.

* * *

I stepped in and the smell of musty books was immediately familiar. But Frank had decorated in here, too. Rearranged the furniture. And although his antique desk was still there, not much else was.

It was that damn smell, though. The old books. Instant recall of the misery inflicted upon me. The hallway was one thing. Frank's room was something else.

Once, when I was eight years old, I came in here to tell Frank that dinner was ready. Dashing with innocent, youthful enthusiasm. But I'd accidentally tripped on my loose laces. Crashed into the desk. His glass of wine had gone over, spilling dark red Merlot all over the paper in which he was contemplating the daily crossword.

I quickly tried to move things around and rescue them from the flood of wine. But Frank grabbed my right arm and yanked me away with too much force.

"You stupid little shit!" he screamed. "*Get out!*"

He was so rough, he dislocated my shoulder.

I quickly pushed aside the memory. I was already feeling an anger beginning to boil. And I couldn't let it.

I looked at Frank's desk. And I saw exactly what I needed to see.

* * *

I walked across the room and sat in his chair. There was a folder open in front of me. It was one of Frank's and it was from his office. I leaned forward and took a closer look at the file.

Jesus, I thought.

This was just what I needed.

The folder was open at the patient's personal details. There was a large colour photograph. The man in the picture was smiling a big happy smile, holding his young son in a playful lift. But a biro had been taken to the smile. The teeth were all blacked out.

I looked at the name in the file and felt my guts turn.

It was DCI Rodney Lucas.

* * *

I dashed from the house. To the Mustang. Started the engine, shoved it into first and roared away.

Lucas lived on the opposite end of town. I'd memorised his address from the file. It would take me about twenty minutes to get there.

I put my foot down.

* * *

Lucas lived in a cul-de-sac of semi-detached houses. Behind his house was a children's play area, so I knew I should approach from there. I got out of the Mustang; cut through an alley to the playground. Counted off the houses. Ducked behind a fence.

And I was in the back garden.

* * *

The window into the kitchen. I saw it all. Lucas, his wife, two boys - roughly twelve and eight years old. Bound to chairs and gagged. Arranged so that the parents faced their children. Eyes all bulging with terror.

But where was Frank?

I crept closer the house for a better look.

A masked figure was pacing around the kitchen, slapping the head of a rusty hammer into the palm of the other gloved hand. The figure was wearing white overalls that were covered with dark splotches of dried blood and brain. Big black work-boots. A pair of cheap-looking pink fairy wings. A pouch clipped to the belt at his waist.

But the worst thing was the mask.

A dirty white cloth bag with large and uneven eye-holes cut into it. A terrible smile, drawn on and filled with a crazy excess of perfectly straight drawn-on teeth. The 'lips' smeared with bright red lipstick.

It was horrible. The grin of total madness.

Lucas was looking at The Tooth Fairy. Watching carefully for any sudden movements. Perhaps weighing up the situation in his mind, assessing things with his unique perspective on the matter. Analysing, absorbing himself in carefully noting reactions, biding his time. Waiting for an opportunity. The problem, though, was that my step-father was fucked in the head. Lucas may not have had time. So, I had to do something. And it had to be now.

* * *

There was no other access to the kitchen than that window. And I didn't have time to fuck about. If I fucked about, lives would have been lost.

I backed up down the garden and I ran at the window. Launched myself into a dive, fists first. I went through the window with a loud smash. Landed in a heap on the kitchen table. The table collapsed on impact and I thudded to the tiled floor. Crockery and cutlery went smashing and crashing around the kitchen. I felt a mild disorientation, nothing else.

I sprang to my feet and eyeballed Frank.

"Trick or treat, fucker!"

* * *

Frank suddenly sprang at me. He was silent, with the hammer raised, ready to split my face in two. I saw the hammer and ducked. But as Frank lunged, he slammed his elbow into my back. I felt the painless thudding blow. It knocked the air from my lungs. The force of it sent me sprawling. Although I was in no pain, I was momentarily disadvantaged.

Frank moved quickly. I felt a heavy work boot stomping on my left leg. I thought I heard something crunch, but wasn't too sure. The intention had clearly been to immobilise me. And although I felt something not right there, I knew in that moment I had to act. I flipped myself round, facing upwards. Kicked out with my other leg. My boot returning the favour.

Frank's knee gave with an audible crack. He cried out, dropped the hammer. Doubled over.

And there was something a bit strange about his yelp. Something not quite *Frank*.

I scrambled to my feet. Frank, bent over, saw the knife amongst the debris on the floor before I did. He snatched it up, stood straight and jabbed it into my chest, slightly off centre. The resistance from the metal plates took him entirely by surprise. The knife went nowhere, his arm painfully jolted by the sudden impact. He dropped the knife and it clanged to the floor.

I made a fist. Punched Frank right in the middle of his face. His bad leg buckled, and he fell on his arse. The pouch on his belt came off and a handful of loose teeth scattered across the kitchen floor. I snatched up the hammer. He needed to be stopped, once and for all. And with a good hard crack to his temple, Frank slumped back. A splotch of blood erupted from inside and sprayed into the fabric of his cloth mask.

I looked at the heap of murdering sick bastard below. Dropped to one knee, leaned down and whipped off his mask. I wanted to spit in his face. But the surprise I felt when I saw the face looking back at me was so intense the tears were in my eyes before I knew it.

"Mum?"

* * *

Her eyes were glazed marbles and there was the vaguest touch of a smile on her lips. She whispered into the tense silence.

"Jack?" Her voice was weak but we all heard it.

"It's me, Mum," I said, removing my hat and mask.

I looked at her. Waited for a response.

But there was none.

Thirteen

I was unmasked. And I was suddenly very aware of it. DCI Lucas, his wife and two children were looking at me. The last tear I would ever shed for this woman fell from my cheek and splashed upon her own. I stood, hat and mask in hand. Turned to face them.

Lucas grunted and struggled against his restraints.

I got the message.

I stepped over to the family and started by untying Lucas. He wriggled himself free and went to the aid of his children, whilst I untied his wife. Presently, I stood back from them. I watched as they hugged each other. Looked at them, as they looked back, eyes red from crying, and unsure what to make of me.

* * *

Lucas released his family and stepped forward, stopping just a foot or two away from me. He looked me right in the eye and nodded gently.

"Thank you," he said. His voice was hoarse.

I nodded back, and looked down. I felt bad for him. I also felt bad for myself. His duty was clear, whether in uniform or not.

I looked back up. He was rubbing his forehead, eyes shut, deep in thought. Soon, he turned to look at his wife. "Take the kids upstairs," he said.

An unspoken communication went between them. She glanced at me then back at him.

– *Will you be okay?*

He replied with a gentle nod.

His wife ushered the kids from the kitchen and I heard their footsteps on the stairs.

Lucas watched them go then turned back to me. "You're Jack Jones?"

"I am," I said.

"From Robert Mitchell and Co?"

"That's right," I said.

He nodded. Then he went back to thinking. He turned his back on me, walked away, then back towards me again.

"All right," he said. "This is what's going to happen. You saved our lives and for that, I owe you. But for the things you've been doing as this Revengelist, I should lock you up. Trouble is, in all good conscience, I can't do that now. You like board games, Mr Jones?"

"Erm… I like Cluedo," I said, not sure where he was going with this.

He nodded. "I like Monopoly. My *kids* like Monopoly, and thanks to you I get to play it with them again. So, this is *your* Get-Out-Of-Jail-Free card, Mr Jones. Your only chance."

He paused. I think it was for dramatic effect.

"When I've finished, you go. You get the hell out of here, and I give you my word you will hear no more about this."

"Okay," I said, expecting more.

"But on two conditions," he said. "Firstly, you get a new job. Understand? You pack *this* shit in, and quit your job with Mitchell's. I don't want to see you down the police station ever again and I *never* want to hear about the fucking Revengelist."

I nodded. "Understood."

"Secondly," he said, "you have nothing more to do with Rachel Slater. She's a good copper. And a nice girl. If she ever found out your secret, it could be the ruin of her. Understand?"

That was a lot harder to swallow. I liked Rachel. I liked her a lot. I really didn't want to do this, but I knew it was the right and proper thing to do. I had faced that realisation some time ago.

I turned to leave. "I understand."

"One more thing, Mr Jones."

I turned back to him. He looked at my hat and mask. I held them up, and saw what he meant. I pulled on the mask. The hat.

"Thanks," I said.

Lucas stuck his hand out.

We shook.

* * *

It was about midnight when I got home. I was exhausted. I broke open a beer, necked it in a few big gulps. Then I stripped, went upstairs and went to bed.

* * *

The first thing I did on waking was to find my anti-bacterial hand scrub. My hands were itching with filth. I cleansed them, rubbing my hands together distractedly as I walked to the bathroom. I took a piss, and washed my hands. I ran the hot water until it was steaming, and squirted soap into my palms – once, twice, three times.

I went downstairs and made coffee and sat at the kitchen table, thinking.

There was so much to think about. My thoughts jumped around from subject to subject, settling on one for no longer than a couple of seconds or so. My mind was like the whooshing chaos of the London Underground.

But this is what I could make sense of.

* * *

I'd inherited the analgesia from Dad. But what from Mum? What kind of defect had she given me? Genetic or otherwise. Because in life, she'd been more than just a loveless mother. Had my gift from her been some sort of mental deficiency? Was I as fucked up as *her*?

Lord knows, I was now a murderer. I'd killed two people in pursuit of what seemed right. And if the truth be told, I wasn't really too upset that one of those was my own mother.

Was that wrong? Did it *matter* that I didn't feel anything about it? She'd been a terrible presence in my life, failing to protect me from an abusive step-father. Failing even to give a shit. But she was still my mother. She was the woman who'd bought me into the world. Didn't that mean I should have felt *something*?

Yet I didn't.

Mum had *clearly* been mental. A twisted psychopath. She'd targeted families and children. She hated them and kept their teeth as souvenirs. But it seemed quite possible she'd given me a generous helping of serious mental problems. I knew I was capable of feeling anger. I knew I was capable of sexual attraction. But what about sympathy? What about remorse?

My actions so far seemed to have been driven from a sense of rage. A sense of frustration at the injustice of criminals avoiding punishment. But I hadn't really thought twice about the things I'd done to people. Reginald Chesterfield. Mick Miller. Johnny Clayton.

These were brutal actions, and yet I felt nothing. Justice was flawed, for sure, but was that enough to justify the things I'd done? To justify murder? To justify a morality that rationalised power and brutality?

As members of a society that values democracy and all the benefits of such, we delegated justice to a higher authority. We empowered the police, the courts and judges. We were expected to play ball with the system. If we didn't like what happened, we had to lump it or vote elsewhere. Vigilante justice *had* to be frowned on by society. The burden of proof in court was a strict one and a jury couldn't convict unless they were sure.

Vigilantes had no rules. Not like the justice system designed by those we put in power. And this was potentially disastrous. There was no objective standard, just personal belief and easily satisfied hunches. And history was clear; acting on rumour was dangerous. Evidence and proof were crucial and without it, the unjust consequences I got into criminal defence for in the first place would ensue. People hounded and punished and reputations ruined because of mistaken belief. Lynch mobs with pitch forks were unacceptable. Hunch wasn't enough for the courts so why should it be for anyone else?

* * *

But sure, society delegated the job of seeking justice to others. Yes, vigilantism was looked upon unfavourably. But mostly by those empowered to deal out justice; those higher authorities that drafted legislation in the interests of society, or the police who conducted investigations, or the courts who tried defendants.

In the main, they were probably right. Criminal laws were written with the right intentions. Some behaviours needed controlling. And the police *tried*, but they were so overwhelmed with work and so seriously understaffed, that too many fuck-ups were allowed to happen. And it wasn't just that. I dealt with coppers who were lazy and under-prepared. They didn't keep up with the law, which affected the efficiency of their investigations.

But it got no better. Jobs in the police force were being slashed left, right and centre whilst the public's need for reassurance was never greater. The impact on victims was terrible. And the government were making the problems worse.

Some rotten bastard with a red pen was going through the figures with a keen eye for saving money. In a society where the concept of justice is one of the key elements of maintaining civilised behaviour, then money shouldn't be a factor. If money is more important than justice, then there's no fucking hope.

As for the courts, their stupid mistakes were beyond *our* control.

So, with all this in mind, did buying into a democratic society mean we had to suffer the god-awful rottenness of people who couldn't give a shit about the rights of others? Did it mean that when some bastard broke into our house, we had to suffer the injustice of watching them leave court with a big smile on their face because the judge didn't send them to prison?

The system was the only system we had, but that didn't mean it was a good system. It didn't mean I had to sit back and watch it all get fucked up through incompetence, disinterest or greed.

Was I mad?

Yes, I probably was.

Was I going to quit my job?

Yes, I would quit my job. My job with Robert Mitchell.

But would I quit my *other* job?

No, I fucking wouldn't.

I was clearly different to most people. I'd built a career looking at information that few had access to. I was experienced enough to see when the evidence was strong enough, and the defendant's explanation so piss poor that I could *deduce* guilt. My education and experience mattered. My willingness to do something was being embraced by people, and so it should have been. It needed doing, and I had what it took to do it.

Anyway, I had one more job to take care of. And although I'd promised DCI Lucas, my work was bigger and more meaningful than a handshake with some copper who had his own motive for making me stop.

* * *

Rupert Bond lived several miles out of town. An isolated house in the sticks. He was a country gent. But he was also a crook.

Clayton *had* been in Harry's house. I *knew* it. The alibi put forward in his interview was false. And knowing Bond as I did, I was certain he'd come up with it. Something substantial enough to make the police bail him for further enquiries. Something flimsy enough that they wouldn't have been able to corroborate it.

Bond *was* a crook. No better than the scum he lied for. He'd perverted the course of justice. And that was a serious criminal offence.

* * *

LOCAL LAWYER INVESTIGATED
Police Examine Claims of Dishonesty as
"Revengelist" Strikes Again

Police have been compelled to launch an investigation into claims that criminal defence lawyer Mr Rupert Bond of Bond, Jenkins & Coleridge Solicitors, assisted criminal suspects to lie. Known by some as "The Devil's Advocate", Rupert Bond allegedly built an "underground" following of criminal clients for his reputation of never losing. Police are now looking into claims that he systematically perverted the course of justice in over two thousand criminal investigations by helping his clients fabricate instructions amounting to legal defences.

This comes just days after self-named vigilante The Revengelist broke into Mr Bond's home. A source close to the police informs us that the vigilante secretly tape-recorded a discussion in which Mr Bond confessed his role.

However, Mr Bond was subsequently subjected to an assault in which his lips were stitched together and dowsed in vinegar. He is currently receiving hospital treatment and the police are of course, eager to question him.

* * *

I spent a few days sorting things out. I wrote to Robert and explained that I wasn't coming back to work. He rang me, confused and angry.

"I don't get it," he said. "I spent a lot of money training you, Jack. Why are you doing this to me?"

"Personal reasons," I said.

"Personal reasons? Have you been offered a job by the competition? Is that it?"

"No," I said.

"You couldn't be doing this to me at a worse time, Jack. Bond and Jenkins are down; their whole firm is in tatters. We're going to be busy here, after Harry went and dropped dead!"

"Goodbye, Robert," I said.

And I hung up.

* * *

I made a start at packing. All my stuff, in bags and boxes. I was leaving town. Leaving Jack Jones behind. A new name, a new start. Lucas might be after me now.

The night before moving there was a knock at my front door. It was about 9pm.

"What the hell is all this about?" It was Rachel. I'd written to her too, and she was waving my letter in the air.

I sighed, and invited her in.

* * *

We were in the kitchen. Rachel was quoting from my letter.

"You've had a lot going on in your life recently? You're not ready for a relationship? You're moving on? What the hell?"

I looked at her. I understood her anger. She liked me, I got that, and she wanted answers.

"Look," I said. "It's really not that easy to explain."

"Yes, it is," she said. "It's actually quite simple. You just open your mouth and don't lie!"

I didn't want to do this. She put the letter down. Thought for a moment.

"Jack, you remember I told you about that guy I nearly married?"

"I do," I said.

"He was living a double life. I found out two days before the wedding. He had a whole family somewhere else. Another house, another wife and two children that loved him. He even had another name. He'd lied to me for two years, Jack. Two years I thought I knew this guy. And it all turned out the joke was on me."

I didn't know what to say.

"He was a con-artist. He'd been trying to rip me off because I had some money stashed away."

I looked at her. "What happened?"

She sighed. "I got in touch with his wife. Put her straight. It ripped that poor family apart. *He* went inside but even now his wife and I keep in contact. We email each other. He'd done it before and when everything got found out, the shit hit the fan."

I was silent. Thinking. I felt bad for her.

"Trust me, Jack. Honesty, I can take. It's the lies I can't."

A double life. Too many lies. Their destructive power was clear.

"What's going on, Jack? Tell me."

* * *

"It's you," I said.

Rachel blinked. Surprised. "Okay," she said. "That's a start, but what does it mean?"

"I haven't been *lying* to you. But I haven't told you all there is to tell. And I *can't* tell you even now. You just have to understand that I'm moving away and it's because of you."

"Do you like me, Jack? Do you have *any* feelings for me?"

I nodded. "That's what makes it worse. But I can't be with you. There are things I still need to do, and if I stayed to be with you, you might..."

She waited a moment. Then she shook her head, not understanding. "I'd what?"

"I don't know. You'd be in danger. You'd stop me. But maybe you wouldn't, and that's worse. I'm not sure. I'm trying, Rachel. It's not easy."

"Okay," she said. "Look, I'm just going to the ladies' room. By the time I get back, you'll have had time to think about what you want to say."

Rachel picked up her handbag. She went upstairs to the bathroom.

She was only gone a minute when the doorbell went.

* * *

My mind was a fucking circus. I didn't know how to deal with this.

I went to the front door and opened it.

A man was standing on the doorstep. His back to me. When he heard the door open, he turned.

"Hello, Jack!"

Frank was smiling, but the shark-like grin was far from friendly. There was a desire to hurt me lurking deep within those eyes.

"What do you want?" I said.

He gestured with one wave of a hand and in a sing-song voice he said, "Oh, whatever's on offer. A cup of tea, a glass of beer, a bit of friendly family cheer."

I thought of Rachel.

"It's not a good time," I said. I glanced past him to the drive. Mine was the only car in sight. Rachel must have come by cab.

"Let me in," he said. The friendly fakery disappeared.

Frank raised his other hand. I saw the gun before he even pointed it at me.

* * *

"It's been *too* long," he said, walking in behind me. "You should have invited your mother and me for dinner. She'd have liked that."

I was in the hall. My back to him.

"In the lounge," he said.

I went through to the lounge. Turned to face him. Frank stuck the gun in my face, at arm's length. There was no pretence now. His face had a hateful, murderous look. The look of a maniac in a third-rate teen-slasher.

I knew that look.

"You were always such a cocky little shit, weren't you, Jack? Always thought you were better than me, didn't you?"

I said nothing.

"No pain, no gain," he said. "Now there's a piece of wisdom you'll never understand, eh?"

I said nothing.

"At first, I didn't get it," he said. "The break-in at my office. But when I found out the alarm had been disabled with its own code, I knew. But I kept quiet. And *that* was a mistake. Because you came back, didn't you? Only when you did, you killed my dog, you fuck!"

So, Brutus was dead. No big loss.

Frank's eyes watered. A single tear trickled down his cheek.

"It was as much a surprise to me as it was to you, Jack. I didn't know your mother was a murdering fucking whore. Maybe I should have seen it. But love is blind, Jack. You don't see those things, because you don't expect to. When you love someone, like I loved her, you'd do anything, you get me? You have to invest something in it. She deserved every broken bone and black eye I gave her, you understand? She needed sculpting. A few good nudges, to bang out the quirks. But you? You were just a worthless little shit."

"I was just a kid," I said.

Frank wiped away the tear with the back of his other hand.

"You were a smug bastard! *That's* what you were. And I won't be trying to hurt you tonight, Jack. I'm going to blow your fucking head open. All over this nice rug."

He glanced down at the nice rug.

I moved quickly. I stepped to one side and grabbed the gun. Frank, although taken by surprise, wouldn't let it go. We wrestled for it. But it was useless. We both had a solid grip on it.

I kicked him hard in the bollocks. He yelped and sank to his knees. He released the grip on the gun and I snatched it from him. Thumped him on the top of his head with the butt and he went down. I made the mistake of thinking he was out. As I stepped over him, he grabbed my legs and tripped me. I fell, dropping the gun. He scrambled over me, grabbed up the gun and stood over me.

"You rotten little cunt!" he snarled.

I cringed. Ready for death. Ready for my brains to explode all over my own lounge floor. But it didn't happen. Instead, I heard a voice.

"*Stop!*"

It was Rachel. She was in the lounge doorway.

I heard Frank. "Who the fuck are *you*?" He sounded desperate.

Then I heard police sirens. Could see flashing blue lights from outside. They were on the drive.

"I'm with them," she said.

* * *

Rachel had been in the bathroom when Frank arrived and she'd heard enough of what was going on to alert the police from her mobile. But I wasn't sure exactly how much she heard.

The police were long gone now and neither Rachel nor I had touched the wine I'd poured.

"He beat you, didn't he?"

"He wanted to hurt me," I said.

"But he couldn't?"

"I can't feel pain," I said.

Rachel was quiet for a moment. How much of this was she piecing together? How much did she know?

"How bad was it?"

I nodded. "It was bad."

"They didn't love you?"

"Neither of them."

Rachel reached out. I was looking down into my lap, and she touched my chin lightly. Lifted my head. "Jack," she said. "Look at me."

It was almost a whisper. Gentle and reassuring. I looked her in the eyes.

"Justice is served, Jack," she said.

And because she couldn't have understood the implications of what she'd just said, she smiled at me.

Part Two
Rougher Justice

Fourteen

I don't know how I managed to last as long as I did. I was amazed, quite frankly, that I hadn't jumped from a bridge. Or stepped into high-speed traffic. And I reckon I might have done, if I'd taken much more. My boss was a noisy fat pig and he was yelling at me again about a mistake I'd made the week before. I *already* knew that it cost him money. I *already* knew that it had pissed him off. But all this bad noise wasn't helping a fucking thing. The problem was that the wasted-costs order came in the post that morning and it kicked him off all over again.

Chunks of the prawn-mayonnaise sandwich he'd stuffed into his face at lunchtime were clinging to his bristling moustache as though it were a well-used Brillo pad. Every few seconds or so, his raucous outburst launched half-chewed bits all over me. It was fucking disgusting.

I hated him.

"And another thing!" he yelled. "Judge Crompton is an old friend of mine. As well as a wasted-costs order, you made me look like a fucking idiot in open court and in front of *him!*"

I nodded. "I know," I said. "And I'm sorry."

Inside, though, I wasn't sorry. I was very fucking far from it. And I was annoyed about the bollocking because I didn't deserve to be yelled at like this. I screwed up and we all knew it. I certainly deserved to be reprimanded once, and to be told to ensure that this kind of shit didn't happen again. But I didn't deserve to be screamed at all over again by some prawn-loving motherfucker with a bad temper.

Instead of feeling sorry, I couldn't help thinking that if he suddenly suffered a stroke right then, I'd piss myself laughing. I hated him *that* much. He made me feel bad in ways a boss shouldn't. And I was looking down at my lap when it dawned on me that I probably looked like a naughty schoolboy.

My boss sat back in his chair with a loud sigh. He saw me looking down.

"Stop looking so damn pathetic," he said. "Your bollocking's over, but understand *this*. I will be thinking very seriously about deducting a contribution to the wasted-costs order from your salary at the end of the month. And I'm *that* pissed off, I might just do it!"

I nodded again. "Okay," I said.

He waved me away with an impatient flap of the hand. "Close the door on your way out," he said, then picked up some work to make the point that the lecture was finally over.

* * *

I wasn't just thinking about quitting. I wanted to do something big along with it, just to make the point sink in. Sometimes, I thought about hanging myself in my office and leaving a note that said:

Royston,
This is your fault, you nasty fat fuck.

Royston was another narcissistic fucking nut. He wasn't much different to Robert Mitchell and I often wondered how I could have been so unlucky to wind up working for yet another mad bastard.

Sometimes I wished *he* was the one who would die. Nobody needed a twat like him making life miserable.

I was totally fed up. People like him made me sick. Hell, people made me sick FULL STOP. The bastards.

Never underestimate their greed. Never underestimate their savagery and their stupidity and ignorance and blind faith in misinformation. Never underestimate a person's capability to fuck you over if it suits them.

I never did anything to that fat bastard that was intentional. I didn't set out to screw him over. I didn't calculate that awful mess or enjoy its consequences with a sadistic sense of pleasure. It was just a stupid mistake.

My mind just wasn't on criminal defence anymore. That was the truth of the matter. Not the way it should have been. I *was* lazy. I didn't give a shit about the clients and that was a problem which had been plaguing me for a long time. After leaving Mitchell & Co, I'd only fallen back into law because it was what I knew and it was an easy way to make some decent money.

I sat back down behind my desk and placed my hands palm down in front of me. With my eyes closed, I took a few deep breaths because they always said that deep breaths helped. In reality, a good shot of vodka would have helped. Deep breaths might distance you from the trigger of your stress by a few moments, thus allowing you to reflect more rationally on it. They might oxygenate your blood and have a calming effect, right down at a chemical level. But I was on the brink of not giving a toss anymore. All I could think about was running into Royston's room with a samurai sword. Deciding that I didn't want to spend the rest of my life in prison though, I went for the breaths instead.

In, two, three. Out, two, three.

Repeat.

Then I opened my eyes. And you know what? I did indeed feel a little bit distanced from thoughts of inflicting pain on that fat bastard.

I found the file I messed up. Kelvin Grayson was a nineteen-year-old dickhead who was up to his nuts in a shit-storm of robbery charges. On the day of his trial, I got a phone call from the court. The trial was ready to go ahead but one crucial person was missing.

"Where is the barrister you sent for Mr Grayson?" asked the clerk.

The minute I heard *that* my nuts shrivelled up. My belly did a loop-the-loop and the sudden sickening lurch of an anxiety attack. It was a catastrophe for sure, and it never should have happened. When the shit hit the fan, my failure to brief a barrister cost us big. I wasn't likely to live it down. The only thing I could do was ensure that there were no more mistakes. Thin ice was a fucking understatement.

But it *was* against the law for Royston to make deductions from my wages without *my* agreement. He said this sort of thoughtless shit all the time. He believed in his power to intimidate me just a little too much.

Dumb cunt.

* * *

I was filled with so much hate and so much anger, I began to think it couldn't be healthy. Or maybe it made no difference. You hear people spout this kind of hippie crap all the time, and you can't help picking it up. You actually start to believe it.

They say it eats you up from the inside. Like a cancerous lump, pulsating and festering at the very core of you. But then again, perhaps hate was a great motivator. Maybe it was right that people actually *were* awful, and every time they let me down it made the hate worse. Maybe bottling the hate up was the problem, not the hate itself. Christ knows, people were never going to change.

I've considered my feelings towards people a lot over the years. And when it all boils down to simple facts, the problem with people can be defined as follows:

1) People are taught from an early age to value self-worth.

2) Self-worth becomes the motivation for self-improvement.

3) Self-worth and self-improvement form the determination to survive. To value the existence of the self, and to form the central "right" to not be prevented from existing or achieving self-improvement.

4) The understanding that all others possess the same values.

5) The understanding that all others therefore pose a potential risk, in possessing those same values, to your own values.

6) The mistrust of others at a deep and fundamental level.

7) The devaluing of others' values in relation to our own.

I fully accept that there are plenty of people who do charitable things, which may on the face of it suggest that I am wrong.

But I'm not wrong.

Plenty of pessimists say that people only do charitable acts because in some way or other, whether large or small, it benefits the person doing them. It probably is the case that anyone who does something charitable feels good about themselves for helping other people. And why not? They're fucking entitled to, I think.

Charity is one of those things you don't automatically or instinctively understand. You don't have an *instinctive* compassion for others in the world who need things more than you might. It's something you have to be educated about, and something you have to learn to care for. Children don't instinctively share. It's something they have to be taught is what society expects of them. And as you age, the lessons in sharing expand. They widen to encompass people who live *without* on a much bigger scale than Lego blocks. You have to *learn* that they possess the same self-worth, the same desires for self-improvement, and don't have the means to facilitate it. Those in a better position can therefore assess the situation intellectually and reach the logical conclusion that it is a good thing to give to those who have nothing, and in reality it doesn't actually matter if you feel good about doing it.

But don't give me all this bullshit that the existence of charity *negates* the suggestion that humans are self-motivated entities and, to some extent, inherently selfish. They are, and that's all there is to it in exactly the same way that no matter how you look at it, 2 + 2 will never equal 5.

Oh, say some people. Well, 2 + 2 *could* equal 5 if you wanted it to. If you *believed* it did, then that is the only thing that matters, isn't it?

No, it is not the only thing that matters. Truth matters too, and 2 + 2, even if you believed it, does not make 5. Whether you believe that people aren't selfish and that the existence of charity (and other things) proves this, you're wrong. The inescapable fact is that like 2 + 2, humans are, at the very core of their nature, self-driven organisms. All the good stuff they do arises from intellectual reasoning rather than a change in the fundamentals of human nature.

* * *

In order to bring myself completely up-to-date, I finished typing up a brief for Kelvin Grayson. I'd already phoned ahead and booked a barrister for the new trial date three weeks away. I *knew* someone would be there this time, and if they weren't, it wouldn't be my fucking fault.

I ended up staying late as usual, but in the end it was all good. Job done. Breathe a sigh of relief.

It was time to go home and get drunk.

Fifteen

Every now and then I checked back into my old email account. There was always this nagging itch to peek. The long-reaching shadow from my past clung to the new life I had forged for myself like shit to a blanket.

It had all just been an epic failure. The last night in town, three years ago. The night Frank came to my house intending to blow my brains out, with Rachel listening upstairs the whole time.

The night I knew that Rachel knew.

"Justice is served, Jack," she'd said, smiling reassuringly.

And it all came crashing down. A fucking disaster.

Rachel's integrity had been paramount and I screwed it all up. Vigilantism was a moral wrangle, for sure. But the authorities just seemed to screw *everything* up. Justice was a bad joke. Faith in their abilities was the punch-line and we were the laughingstock.

The Revengelist was born of a need to satisfy some messed-up and self-serving desires, sure, but also to serve the needs of the people. Yet I corrupted the person I loved. The person whose seemingly immovable moral values were the one thing I had to try to protect. The one thing I had vowed not to do had happened anyway, and for that reason, I failed.

But as The Revengelist, I *did* serve some good. I caught and killed a psychopathic serial killer, who of course turned out to be my own twisted mother.

I saved a family just minutes before their terrible slaughter. I exposed a sick rapist who filmed his crime and blamed the victim.

And I helped lock up a child-abusing, gun-wielding maniac who hid behind a façade of upstanding decency.

But the whole thing was hard to let go of. I'd done some good. It was undeniable. The buzz I felt thinking about it was addictive. And every couple of months or so I logged in to my email account, just out of curiosity. Just in case there was something there. Mostly, it was full of crap. My spam folder was always clogged up with the kind of subject headings you didn't give a shit about. Insurance, dating sites. Some foreign beneficiary who needed your bank account details.

But one day there was something unexpected. There was an email from 'Rachel N. Slater' with the subject heading: *Please Read This.*

When I saw it, my first instinct was to delete it.

Highlight, delete.

Easy.

But Rachel obviously had something she needed to say. Something that she thought was urgent. And I couldn't delete it.

I returned to my inbox several times, looking at the unopened email and wondering what it said. Wondering why Rachel felt the need to contact me after all that had happened. After leaving the way I did. Wondering why I was so reluctant to open it, yet also reluctant to delete it.

The existence of this email nagged at me for days. A mouth ulcer you can't stop poking with your tongue no matter how much it hurts.

And eventually of course, I buckled to the curiosity and opened the damn thing.

I was pretty sure in my belief that what we thought of as the past was nothing more than the private memories of every separate individual. There was no *collective* past. No place where the whole of humanity's history was stored like data on a PC hard-drive. It was all just impulses in the brain and they were not worth obsessing over. Rachel was in *my* past. Everything that had happened between us was gone. It was ruined. I hoped desperately that I had the strength to ensure that the past was where that mess stayed. Some ruins just weren't meant to be rebuilt.

This is what the email said:

Jack,

Please help. Something very bad has happened. Something I think Our Friend should look into, and urgently. Get in touch.

Rachel.

* * *

I had no way of knowing what she meant. But my curiosity was piqued and she probably knew damn well when writing that email that it would be.

But I knew something else, too.

The Revengelist wouldn't be welcome. If Rodney Lucas even got the faintest whiff of my return, he'd be on my arse like a fucking haemorrhoid. I doubted there'd be any point throwing in his face the fact that I'd saved his life. His wife and kids, too. Ultimately, I'd gone against our agreement. And a man who breaks a solemn promise on a gentleman's handshake is a worthless piece of shit.

In the end, I'd done what he wanted. I'd given up my work as The Revengelist. I had no choice. When Frank was arrested that night, the officers had grilled me for a statement and with Rachel at my side, holding my hand in support, the floodgates opened. All my experiences at the hands of that vile fucker.

I told them about my condition. That Mum left Dad and married Frank, and that Frank hated my guts. I told them that they couldn't have kids, and that being incapable of feeling pain made things worse between us. Made him envy me and try harder to hurt me. That he seemed to refuse to be rendered powerless by my gift from Dad.

I told them about Gran, and her death. Her note to me and the inheritance. I told them that I found out Mum was sneaking into people's houses, tying them up and battering them to death with a hammer.

I told them I found out that she was the one that people called The Tooth Fairy and that shortly after, Frank turned up at my house with a gun and tried to shoot me.

I told them I'd been dating Rachel and that she happened to be upstairs at the time, and that Frank hadn't known this when he turned up.

I told them everything, except, of course, that I was The Revengelist. That had to remain my little secret...

But actually, it wasn't just mine. Rachel knew about it too, and she sat there with me and said nothing. She held my hand. Comforting me. Supporting me. Steadily losing the integrity I'd placed so much importance on. Withholding crucial information from these officers who probably trusted her implicitly.

Her silence decided many things. It decided that Rachel had abandoned the principles for which she was known. The decency. The honesty.

It also decided that as well as being a dishonest copper, she was now a criminal, too. She knew about me. She knew the things I'd done and was withholding that information from the police. Willing to make a statement to deflect attention.

She was perverting the course of justice, and she would have to go to court and give evidence and swear on oath that what she was saying was the truth, the whole truth and nothing but the truth.

Her path was chosen.

* * *

Frank was charged with attempted murder. He was remanded into custody and taken before the magistrates, who bounced his case (by virtue of it being indictable-only) straight up to the Crown Court.

At the first hearing, he pleaded not guilty. I did some sniffing around, and it turned out that his solicitor was some fuck from Bond, Jenkins & Coleridge. It wasn't Rupert Bond, of course. Bond was on a suspension pending the outcome of the police investigation.

It was fairly obvious Bond would walk away from it all. The only evidence the police had against him was the tape-recording I made when I tortured him and got his confession. That wouldn't be worth a damn if no one made a statement against him, and who the fuck would do *that*? The only people who were in a position to were the very same ones he'd spared a long haul inside.

No. The Devil's Advocate would get away with his crimes scot-free. I knew that. He'd be back with Bond, Jenkins & Coleridge in no time.

Before then, though, Frank's solicitor was Isaac Harper. The brief went to a good barrister. But once a jury were sworn in, I knew that it didn't matter who his barrister was. Frank could have been represented by Perry fucking Mason but he still wouldn't stand a chance. They'd squeeze my bottled-up past like puss from an angry boil, and that mad bastard would go down.

All the lawyers in the world couldn't save him, whether they were honest or not. And I would be left with no sense of purpose or direction.

* * *

But what of Rachel? The last time I saw her was outside the Crown Court. Not long after she'd given the evidence which hammered the final nail in Frank's coffin. The evidence not only of an independent witness, but of an off-duty police officer.

It was never going to be disbelieved.

And so, as I stood at the foot of the court-house steps, sipping coffee and thinking about what to do with my life, she walked out of the revolving door and gathered her coat against the chilly February wind.

I watched her descend the steps, and she stopped in front of me. Cheeks flushed, breath puffing out. Her frame was hunched against the weather, her eyes watery from the bitter cold.

Or was I just telling myself that? Was it more likely that she was angry, and hurt and struggling to come to terms with lying on oath for me?

"Thank you," I said to her.

She nodded. "I don't think the jury will buy his self-defence crap," she said.

I agreed with her. Frank's defence was piss poor. He said he'd come to the house to confront me, believing me to be The Revengelist. Although he never knew that Mum was The Tooth Fairy, he said he was sure I'd broken into his home and killed his dog to get even for the child-abuse I'd always claimed to be the victim of (which he also denied). He said he never took the gun with him. It was *me* who produced the gun, and threatened to kill *him* and that he had to fight me in order to wrestle the gun from me. That *this* was what Rachel saw when she came into the lounge.

"No," I said. "Neither do I."

There was a pause. An awkward silence. Rachel was the one to break it.

"Are you sticking around to hear his evidence?" she asked.

I sniffed against the cold. "No, I don't think I'll bother. I'm heading off soon; I just wanted to make sure I saw you one last time."

Rachel smiled politely. "You *are* welcome you know," she said. "You don't need to harp on about it."

"I just didn't want to leave with you thinking…"

Rachel lifted her eyebrows, inquisitively. "What, that you're some weirdo?"

I shrugged. "I was thinking more along the lines of arsehole, actually."

She chuckled. "Ain't much gonna change that!"

I smiled at her. I always did like her humour. But sometimes certain things had to be said and not kept bottled up.

"I *do* have to go, you know. I hope you understand. I made a deal with someone and broke it. It was the kind of deal you're meant to take seriously, and for that reason, I can't stick around."

Rachel nodded, but I could see on her face that she was still hurt. Still not convinced.

"Well," she said. "I guess we *both* better get going. I've got a life to get back to and you've got a new life to start. I would say I'll see you around but I guess that's bullshit."

She sniffed. Hunched up even tighter against the cold. Then she turned and walked away.

"Rachel?" But it was hopeless even trying.

Without turning, she said, "Goodbye, Mr Jones."

And that was when the cold drew tears from *my* eyes, too.

* * *

Frank was convicted. He put on a good show, but there was just no evidence connecting me to The Revengelist. No one was ever going to buy it. So, when it came to sentencing, the judge took the following points into account:

1) Frank had no previous convictions, but conviction after trial *never* went well for anyone.

2) Frank had obviously intended to murder me and *he* took the gun to my house.

3) He also obviously intended to use the gun, evidenced by my own and Rachel's account that he said, "I'm going to blow your fucking head open. All over this nice rug."

Frank was a danger to the public, said the judge, and locked him away with immediate effect. If Frank was ever lucky enough to get himself released, it wouldn't be for a *very* long time. By then, he'd just be a doddery old cunt.

* * *

My feelings for Rachel never changed. Not at any point during the court case. Not when I saw her outside court that day, cold and tearful. Not on any single day that followed for the three years after. I missed her. But I knew that the ruins of our past must never be rebuilt. Not if it meant digging the knife in further. Not if it meant entangling her in my double life.

She'd been down the road of double lives before, and it bought her heartache. True, the difference with that other fucker was that he was after money. He didn't care about Rachel's feelings. I did. And that was precisely why I couldn't even contemplate contacting her. She was in enough shit and it didn't need to get any worse.

But when that email came, it changed everything. She was asking for help. And that put a different spin on things.

* * *

As I sat at my laptop, looking at the email from Rachel, I couldn't help but wonder where this would take me. If I sent the response, I was thinking about sending, what sequence of events would it trigger? What kind of trouble would I get myself into? Could it all go wrong enough to land me in prison alongside Frank?

I had no way of knowing. But one thing I did know was that the woman I cared about had asked for my help. I could hardly turn that down.

I drafted my email, and then sat back and looked at it.

Rachel,
Whatever has happened, I think Our Friend is best left out of it. Can you tell me what the problem is, then we can figure out a way forward.
Jack.

It seemed a bit curt, but after a few moments of internal debate, I leaned forward, rolled the cursor over *send* and punched it in.

Job done.

* * *

It took less than fifteen minutes for Rachel to respond. Being a Sunday, I didn't know whether she was on duty, but it seemed she wasn't. She was emailing from her iPhone (a footnote in the email said as much), and I figured that if she had been at work she'd have been too busy to be sending emails from her phone.

This is what her response said:

Jack,
Meet me tomorrow at ten am. There's a café in town called Gav's... a greasy spoon. I'll be waiting for you, so make sure you come and I'll explain everything. Our Friend will be perfectly safe, trust me.
Rachel.

There was a very clear and desperate edge to her email. Something *was* wrong. Something bad, too, by the sound of it. But what? What was so bad that she had to set up a meeting like this, all cloak-and-dagger? And could I be so sure that I'd be safe? How could she vouch for that?

Rodney Lucas was no doubt still mad at me. If he knew I was floating around town *and* meeting with Rachel, I'd be for it. How could I not be? What did she *know* that I didn't to assert the reassurance that I'd be safe?

Too many fucking questions, and too few answers.

I resigned myself to accepting that I'd find out in the morning and quickly typed out an acknowledgement.

Okay, Rachel. Tomorrow at ten, Gav's.
Jack.

And then I hit send.

Sixteen

I phoned work the following morning at about 7.30am. I left a message on the answer machine that said I was feeling ill. To not expect me in for a couple of days. If I lost my job, then I lost my job. I was sick of that fat fucker Royston, anyway.

I still had my Revengelist clobber. I had the Mustang, and I had my outfit. It was all safely stored in a rented garage. No one had seen me put it all away, but it wouldn't have mattered if they had. I'd moved away from the city a few years ago. The Mustang wasn't just the vehicle of choice for night-prowling vigilantes. *Other* people owned them, too. I sometimes had to remind myself of that. Just because I knew I was The Revengelist, it didn't mean I gave off a guilty vibe.

But still, I wasn't going to tempt fate by driving the Mustang just yet. I got into my civvie car and headed into the city.

* * *

There was a car-park just around the corner. I parked up, paid for a ticket and casually walked around to Gav's.

I was on a side-street pavement. Not too far from the cluster of main shopping streets and indoor malls. I found Gav's easily. It was a well-presented café, brightly lit. I stepped up to it, opened the door and went in. There were a few customers sitting at tables. They looked up as the bell above the door jingled. I gently closed the door and took a seat, noting immediately that Rachel hadn't arrived yet.

I looked at my watch. Tapped the table-top, thoughtfully. 9.58am.

"I'll be with you in a minute, love!"

A lady behind the counter. Hair tied back. Apron.

I smiled back at her. "That's fine, thanks," I said.

The smells of a cooking breakfast filled the place. Frying bacon. The sound of sizzling from the kitchen behind her. A radio played a local city station. Some DJ who thought he was funny.

I sat facing the front door, side on to the window that looked onto the pavement. That way, I'd see Rachel coming up the street before she came through the door. My back was to the other patrons. A large man with a fluorescent tabard. Shovelling down breakfast, no doubt, before slogging it out on a construction site somewhere. A middle-aged man and woman with a pensioner's shopping cart off to one side. Some old boy drinking tea and eating buttered toast.

And me. But no Rachel. I looked at my watch. 10.00am exactly.

Then I heard someone shuffle up to me.

"All right, love, what'll it be?"

It was the waitress. I turned and looked up at her. She was standing with a pencil poised above a notepad, smiling at me.

"Hi," I said. "Can I just have a coffee, please?"

"Cup or mug, love?"

"Is there a difference?" I said.

Something changed in the way the woman looked at me. It was a look I recognised. A slight drop in *actual* politeness, a vague suspicion briefly replacing it, whilst trying to maintain the smile for the *appearance* of politeness. It was a look that said: *Is he going to be trouble?* But then as quick as it was there it was gone again.

"There is, actually," she said. "A mug is bigger. So, if you want more coffee than a normal cup holds, I'd go for the mug."

I smiled. "That sounds like a plan," I said. "I'll have the mug, please."

The woman nodded her approval. "One mug coming up," she said, and off she went.

I looked at my watch again. Was this getting a bit obsessive? It was only 10.02am. There was still plenty of time for Rachel to get here. And true, I thought she'd be here before me. That when I arrived, I'd find her waiting. Anxious to meet me. I guess I only judged it this way by the tone of her email.

But the fact that I'd arrived first meant nothing. She may have been caught in traffic. And it was still only 10.02am, after all.

But I checked my watch just to make sure.

Now it was now 10.03am.

* * *

The waitress brought the mug of coffee over at nearly ten past. She set it down in front of me.

"Is everything all right?" she said. "I've seen you looking at your watch a few times."

"Fine," I said. "I was supposed to meet someone here but she appears to be running late."

"Ah!" she chirped. It made me jump. "Your name isn't Jack, by any chance?"

She knew my name! Dread in my guts, like a brick.

What could it mean?

Maybe Rachel had phoned ahead. Perhaps she *was* stuck in traffic, and had asked the staff to pass a message on.

Perhaps. But perhaps I was deluding myself. Perhaps she'd had a change of heart and wasn't coming at all. Perhaps I'd made her so miserable she'd had second thoughts about meeting me and decided to stay at home instead. She might have been sitting there right at this *very* moment, looking at her clock. Knowing I'd be here, wondering how long I'd wait before giving up. Knowing that when she *was* satisfied I'd given up, she could relax a little.

How did I deal with this? If I denied being Jack, I may miss something which would put my mind at ease. If I confirmed I was Jack, I may expose myself to a rejection that would make me feel terrible.

Fuck it, I thought.

I looked up at her and smiled. "I *am* Jack," I said. "How did you know?"

She trotted off, back behind the counter. "Coz I knew you were coming," she said. "There's something here for you."

This was sounding even worse.

She came back to my table with an envelope, and handed it to me. "Some bloke came in just after we opened up. He gave me this and said a guy called Jack was going to be here at ten, but whoever you were meant to be meeting isn't going to make it."

I held the envelope. A slim, beige A5. Sealed with a strip of tape. My name handwritten in capitals on the front.

My anxiety levels were up.

"Thank you," I said. "How much do I owe you for the coffee?"

* * *

I took the envelope back to my car and sat behind the steering wheel. I could just imagine what it said. Something about never wanting to see me again, probably. About how she never deserved to be dragged into the nightmare I had dragged her into. About how seeing me again would set off feelings that she didn't want to feel for me again.

A huge part of me didn't want to open it. A voice in my head was telling me to bin it and drive away. To not look back and never even think of returning. To chalk it up as another one of life's mistakes, and just get on with what lies ahead. Sure, I'd feel bad for a while. But such is life. We feel bad, we heal, we move on.

But I did none of those things.

I opened it.

* * *

Inside was a folded piece of A4. When I opened *that*, this is what was written:

Jack,

She ain't coming. So now, the question you gotta ask yourself is why. Is it coz she changed her mind, or is it something else? Is it because no matter how much she may wanna come, she CAN'T? Is she tied and gagged somewhere, in lots of pain?

Bleeding, maybe?

It wasn't signed from anyone, but underneath the printed note was a picture. It looked like this:

* * *

I considered the note, over and over. The blood steadily boiling behind my eyes. The anger rising.

What did it mean? What the *fuck* did it mean?

Someone knew that Rachel was coming to meet me.

That was the starting point. They knew where and they knew when.

They had a reason to prevent the meeting from happening.

That was the second thing. A conscious effort was made to stop the meeting going ahead, and there was some reason for that.

Whoever it was had kidnapped Rachel.

That was the most worrying thing. Whoever wanted to sabotage it had wanted to do so badly enough that they had kidnapped Rachel and, by the sound of it, injured her.

The motherfuckers!

No... They were more than just motherfuckers. They were *dead* motherfuckers!

* * *

This was what I needed to know:

1) Who could have known that Rachel was meeting me?

2) What was the motive for stopping the meeting?

3) Where was Rachel being held?

And what the hell was that horrible fucking skull thing all about?

I didn't know what to do. I could have gone blundering into this whole mess with a brainless, gung-ho stupidity. But that would have probably ended badly. My best option was to go back home. Gather intelligence. Find out who I was going after and get the job done properly.

And *properly* meant only one thing.

It meant suiting up.

Seventeen

The first thing I googled was the city news, looking for any reports of use.

The local rag made one thing clear very quickly. This was not an isolated case. There'd been a spate of kidnappings over the past month or so, all linked by that skull image. A relative of each victim promptly received an envelope and inside the envelope was a note, taunting them with some grotesque and abusive statement of intent.

Every victim was female.

Most disturbing was the appearance of that skull in every single disappearance. Information had leaked to the media, and it transpired that whoever was doing this was some bastard who called himself Skull-Fuck.

Another nick-named nutter. That did not bode well for the future of the victims.

Currently, the six victims were:

1) Thirty-eight-year-old mother of two Claire Edwards.
2) Nineteen-year-old student Lisa Daniels.
3) Thirty-six-year-old employment lawyer Andrea Freeman.
4) Forty-year-old housewife Yvonne Long.
5) Twenty-six-year-old supermarket worker Tanya Maynard.
6) Thirty-seven-year-old advertising executive Olivia Graham.

And, judging by the note I had received, Rachel made seven. The authorities didn't seem to know of her abduction yet. Her name hadn't been mentioned anywhere, but then again, it was probably far too early. And that left me with a slight problem. Did I take what I now knew to the police? Did I report her abduction and risk exposing myself? It wouldn't take the police long to fathom out that she was meeting with me that day. That there was a reason for her to meet with me.

Inevitably, they'd piece it all out. Who I was, what I'd done. But worse than that, they'd also figure out that Rachel *knew*. That she hid it all. That she lied on oath in the Crown Court.

But if I didn't go to the police, something really bad could happen. I couldn't be solely responsible for finding her. And I didn't want to be responsible for anything worse happening, either.

So, what was I supposed to do?

* * *

In the end, it was obvious. If I was going to phone the police, I could have done that sitting in my car just around the corner from Gav's. I was a murderer, for Christ's sake. There was too much at stake, and besides, I was confident I could catch this bastard. He'd left me that note for a reason. He *wanted* to communicate with me, and all I had to do was figure out why.

These fucking nutters seemed to enjoy bragging. They seemed to have something they wanted to say, and someone they wanted to say it to. This fucker clearly wanted my attention. And he'd got it. So, I'd get him. I was confident of that.

It was just a matter of time.

* * *

I logged into my email account and sifted through the messages. Rachel's first message to me was there. It was the one I was looking for.

The date it landed in my inbox was Thursday 7th October. I hadn't opened it until Sunday 10th October. It was about 7pm on Sunday that I replied, and less than fifteen minutes after *that*, Rachel had offered the name of our meeting place. But having been abducted, presumably at some point between 7.30pm and 9am the next morning, just after Gav's opened up, her abductor was able to learn the meeting details and thus sabotage it.

Whoever this Skull-Fuck character was, he was taunting me.

Is she tied and gagged somewhere, in lots of pain?

Bleeding, maybe?

Yes... he was definitely taunting me. But why? And *how* had he known about the meeting?

* * *

I decided to go and retrieve my Revengelist stuff. Before I set off, though, I googled the phone number for Gav's.

"Hello?" It was the woman from earlier.

"Hi," I said. "You may recall me from this morning. You gave me the envelope that someone dropped off at opening time."

"Oh, yeah!" she said. "Is everything all right?" Her tone had shifted and I heard a degree of concern there.

"Yes, fine," I said. "I was hoping to establish who gave you the envelope and with that in mind, perhaps I could be permitted an opportunity to review your CCTV footage?"

"Oh," she said. "We haven't got any CCTV."

Shit, shit, shit!

I thought for a moment. A description wouldn't really help much. But I asked for one anyway.

"Well, he was average height, I suppose. Fairly large build. But he was wearing a woolly hat so I can't really tell you what kinda hair he had. Sorry about that."

"No worries," I said. "Thank you for your help."

With the tone of concern now stepped up to one of suspicion, the woman said, "You *sure* everything's all right?"

"Positive," I said. "Goodbye."

* * *

I walked to my rented garage. I didn't want to drive there and leave my civvie car nearby. It would be a foolish oversight. Perfectly traceable.

The garage was about a mile away and although it was now dark and chilly out, I didn't mind. It gave me time to think. The relative quiet of the streets was only disturbed once, as a carload of yobs went screeching past. Music thumping so loud it distorted and crunched the speakers. One of the kids, with his face pressed up against a half-open window, screamed something at me I could barely understand.

It made me jump, and the car was gone before my shout of "Fuck off and crash!" had even left my mouth.

Calm down, I thought. *Just fucking calm down.*

This whole thing had made me overly jumpy.

The garage was on a patch of land connected to a moderately well-off area. I was worried that if I'd rented it in some breeding-hole of scumbags it would have been broken into by now.

I found my garage and dug out the key from my coat pocket. My breath was puffing out as I stood thoughtfully in front of the corrugated door. The orange halo from a nearby street-light casting its strange, lonely glow.

So, it was pretty much decided, really. I'd promised Rodney Lucas that I'd give up on The Revengelist. And although my final act was to get Rupert Bond and stitch his lips together, I did what I'd agreed to do in the end.

Still. I knew that Lucas wouldn't be too impressed to see me again. My path as The Revengelist had been criminal.

The path I was *now* about to tread was, quite possibly, the path of utter foolishness.

* * *

I drove back into the city in the Mustang. Sitting on the back seat was my suitcase, filled with all the items of my costume. After giving up on the whole thing three years ago, I'd cleaned the suit down. A stiff-bristled brush. Hot soapy water and lots of bleach. A good final blast with a jet-washer.

It was unlikely to bear any incriminating evidence.

I drove carefully, not wanting to do anything that might attract the attention of the police. My eyes kept flicking up to the rear-view mirror. Looking at the suitcase on the seat. The suit inside it had turned me into The Revengelist. The leather in that suitcase had been on my skin when I'd killed and maimed and hurt people.

I felt slightly weird just thinking about it. Not guilt. Not remorse.

It was the pangs of temptation. Or, to be more precise, a kind of excited anticipation. An *eagerness*.

I hadn't been The Revengelist for three years. And although of course, I was the one who had hurt and maimed and killed, it had been all too easy for me to lock that part with the costume in the suitcase. The Revengelist clearly wasn't a separate entity, and no amount of psycho-babble bullshit would prove it was. But nevertheless. I was still feeling somewhat keen to get this done. Perhaps *too* keen. The Revengelist wasn't separate, but the suit gave me license to do the things that Jack Jones couldn't do. Things that *had* to be done.

Things that hurt.

* * *

By the time I pulled the Mustang into Rachel's street it was about 10pm. I parked up, killed the lights, turned the engine off. Then I sat for a moment. Looking at the house, several yards away. An average three-bedroom semi-detached. There didn't seem to be a single light on anywhere.

Okay, I thought. *Here goes.*

I turned in my seat and reached over the back. Opened the suitcase and rummaged around for the gloves. I pulled them on, then clambered from the car and shut the door as quietly as possible.

Don't mind me. Just an ordinary citizen going about his business.

I walked up Rachel's drive and went straight to the gate on the side which led round to the back garden. I kept my eye on the front room bay-window. I couldn't see anything in there. It was dark. But I had this terrible feeling that a man with a pale white skull would suddenly jump up with blood trickling from the empty eye-sockets. A menacing, toothy grin.

But thankfully, nothing. All seemed clear.

I came to the side gate. Tried it.

It opened.

I stepped quietly down the passage between the house and the side wall and came out into a small back garden. The back door was nothing special. Not one of these newer, PVCu things. It was wooden and not very sturdy looking. Single-pane windows, top and bottom. The top window had been put through and the door was standing ajar.

Rachel had been abducted from her own home.

As I approached the back door, my boots crunched on pieces of broken glass under foot. There wasn't likely to be anyone here. I knew that. But still –

If there was, they'd know I was here *now.*

I reached out and touched the door. Pushed it further open and cautiously stepped into the house.

The kitchen was cold and dark and eerily quiet. Glass crunched beneath my feet again. There was clear evidence of someone having lived here, but no signs of recent occupation. It was just like the Mary Celeste. Unwashed crockery in the sink. Coffee cups, a couple of plates with traces of food encrusted upon them. Magazines and cookery books heaped to one side of her microwave. Post-it notes and scraps of paper pinned to a notice board with reminders of important things. Bills, letters, appointments. An overflowing laundry basket just visible in a utility room off the kitchen.

All the usual things. The normal, mundane things.

But no Rachel.

I felt vaguely as though I was intruding. Like a trespasser. As though she'd just popped out somewhere, and I was the kind of scumbag, opportunistic junkie burglar I defended regularly. It was strangely unpleasant, and it was probably only because it was Rachel's house that I felt this way. Any other piece of criminal dog-shit, and I wouldn't have cared.

It was a little bit like snooping through a loved one's diary. Seeing her unwashed crockery – seeing her laundry basket, spilling over with worn knickers. It felt like I was nosing through her secrets.

I moved further into the house. It was as cold inside as it was out. It felt as though the heating hadn't been on in days.

I was now in the hallway, heading down to the lounge. As I drew closer to her front door, at the end of the hall, I could see a pile of post. Unopened letters, takeaway menus and dross. All the usual bullshit that came through your door on a daily basis. All just lying there, scattered messily across the doormat.

If the other things I'd seen up to now weren't signs that Rachel wasn't here, then this dismal little pile most definitely was. I grimaced at it. At the truth it betrayed.

And when I looked at the lounge doorway, I could see a faint glow illuminating the walls inside. A faint, bluish glow.

I took a breath, half expecting to see Rachel's corpse propped up on the sofa, facing me but seeing nothing. Black, scooped-out eye-holes filled with the dark emptiness of death. A wretched, freeze-frame scream of torment on her cold dead face.

And then I stepped into the lounge.

* * *

I think I was so convinced that this was what I would see that, for a silent split second of complete and utter Hell, it was exactly what I did see. When I blinked, the image was gone. Rachel was not here. Of course, she wasn't. The lounge was as empty as the rest of the house.

Empty of life, anyway. The furniture was all here. I recognised it from the night we came back here together after the Lobster Pot, all those years ago. But there was one noticeable difference.

It was a total fucking mess.

The blue glow I saw from the hallway was Rachel's laptop. It was on a desk at the far end of the room, facing me. It was still on, and in its glow I could see chairs overturned. Tables thrown aside. Newspapers and celebrity-gossip magazines scattered all over.

The place looked like a bomb had gone off.

It was all evidence of some major struggle. It wouldn't have taken Sherlock fucking Holmes to see *that*. Something bad had happened here. And as I waded through the mess, I saw in the bluish glow of Rachel's laptop a few spots of blood on the carpet.

I bent for a closer examination but quickly found that just looking at them and understanding what they meant made me so damn angry I had to tell myself to look away.

She'd been hurt. And I was now in danger of losing my rag.

Big style.

* * *

I looked at the screen of Rachel's laptop. The bright blue ripples of a bog-standard Windows wallpaper. She must have adjusted the settings at some point to prevent the laptop from going into hibernation. To disable the screen-saver, even. And it was still plugged into the mains.

This computer had clearly not been turned off since Rachel's abduction.

If it hadn't been used in that time, then Rachel would have been the last person to use it, and that information would be stored in the computer. Locating it might help me determine when Rachel was abducted.

I sat down at her desk. I reached out and touched the mouse, connected via USB. The cursor moved with it.

Good. No problems there.

I went straight into her control panel, selected *system and security*. Then into *administrative tools* and finally *event viewer*.

I was looking for the last time the computer was booted up. I sifted through all the shit for a while until I finally found it.

Rachel's computer had been running since Thursday 7th October, 18.15 hrs.

* * *

So, what the hell did that mean?

I wasn't entirely sure. It might have meant that Rachel was abducted on the night of the 7th October. But that was the same night I got the email from her that I didn't open. That I didn't open until Sunday 10th when, after replying, Rachel had promptly responded from her iPhone.

Or had she?

This Skull-Fuck had written to me personally. Could it be possible that *he* had sent the emails? That Rachel was sitting gagged and bound somewhere the whole time -

(In lots of pain?)

(Bleeding, maybe?)

- and that this was some sick plan to get *me*?

Or was *that* just a bit narcissistic?

As I was thinking these things, I closed the control panel and I saw an icon on her desktop. It was a jpeg called "Clipping: Claire Edwards".

Claire Edwards?

She was the first of Skull-Fuck's abductees.

I double-clicked the icon and an image-viewer opened. Before me was now what appeared to be a newspaper clipping, scanned into Rachel's laptop. It read as follows:

SEARCH FOR MISSING MOTHER CONTINUES

Police have widened their search today for missing mother of two, Claire Edwards. The thirty-eight-year-old was last seen by friends in Sparklz, a nightclub in the city centre. According to reports, Claire was out celebrating her sister's hen party and was last seen exiting the club to smoke a cigarette. Investigations by the police have so far generated no leads, and they are appealing to anyone who may have information to come forward. Ms Edwards has been described by friends and family as a loving and devoted mother who "never had a bad word to say about anyone". Earlier this month, Ms Edwards' ex-husband, DCI Rodney Lucas, was arrested in the on-going investigation, but was subsequently released without charge.

* * *

DCI Rodney Lucas! What the fuck...?

This whole mess was suddenly beginning to look a bit bigger now.

Eighteen

There was no doubt about my next move. No doubt at all. Rodney Lucas may have considered me the last person he ever wanted to see on his doorstep, but it was now pretty damn unavoidable.

I opened Rachel's internet browser and carried out a few searches. I managed to establish that Lucas still seemed to be living at the address I knew from before.

The house I'd been to three years ago.

The house in which I'd killed my own mother.

I closed the internet then decided, on second thoughts, to go back in and erase my searches from the internet history.

That done, I left Rachel's house and got back in the Mustang.

* * *

The cul-de-sac looked just the way it had on Halloween night three years ago, minus the pumpkin jack-o'-lanterns. I recognised Lucas's house the second I saw it.

It was now about 11pm, but the house was lit up. I took that to mean Lucas was still up, so I walked over to his house. Up his drive. Reached out my hand and knocked on the door.

I heard shuffling. Through the frosted glass in the door, I saw a hunched figure shambling down the hall. Then I heard the lock, the rattle of a chain, and finally the door opened.

The feeling of anxiety in my belly was making me sick. I was making a big mistake. I was sure of it. I was making a terrible mistake.

When I saw Lucas peering at me, I thought I was going to puke on his feet.

But when he clocked it was *me*, he said, "I was wondering when you'd show up."

Then he turned his back and shuffled off down the hall, leaving the front door wide open for me.

* * *

The first thing I noticed was the smell. The house stank of booze and cigarette smoke. I shut the door behind me, and as I turned, I saw Lucas at the kitchen table. He was in a scruffy beige dressing-gown. A grubby vest beneath. There was a cigarette sticking out of his mouth, and he was squinting against the smoke as he poured himself a large measure of whisky.

There was another glass sitting in front of him and he sloshed a good measure into that, too.

I walked down the hallway. Lucas removed the cigarette from his mouth, inhaled with an audible hiss, and blew out smoke. He waved his hand at me impatiently.

"Sit down," he said. "And get that up your guts."

"Thanks," I said. "But I'm driving."

He looked at me. His glare was serious and piercing. "Sit down and fucking *drink*," he said.

There was something very uncomfortable about this. I was pretty sure that I was witnessing the result of some sort of mental breakdown and I didn't want to rock the boat. So, I sat and picked up the glass of whisky. Sipped a small amount.

"Cheers," said Lucas, raising his glass. He knocked his back in one go. Slammed the empty glass down and promptly refilled it. Then he looked up at me.

"Let's get this started," he said.

"I don't know *where* to start," I said feebly.

Lucas gestured with his hands. It was a gesture that said, *here, there, anywhere will do.* "How about we start with Halloween, three years ago?"

And like that, we were into it. It seemed like a good idea to indulge Lucas but my anxiety levels were up. I wanted to take the edge off my nerves. So, I picked up the whisky and gulped it down in one. As though it were a reflex action, he uncorked the bottle, reached over and refilled my glass.

"I made an agreement with you, and then broke it a few days later," I said.

Lucas blew out smoke. "Yep. You fucking did," he said. "And maybe you've been stewing about that these past few years. But look at me, Jack. Do you think I still give a shit?"

I said the first thing that came to mind.

"I'm not sure *what* to think."

Lucas chuckled. "Yeah," he said. "Quite the mess, aren't I?"

I looked down. "Well, I wouldn't say *that*."

"You don't have to," he said. "And the thing is, Jack, there was a time when I felt pretty pissed off about what you did. But I gave it a lot of thought. And you know what I decided?"

I shook my head.

Lucas dragged hard on his smoke. Exhaled loudly. "I decided that the truth of the matter was, I hated that fucking prick as much as you did. And when it all boils down to it, he was asking for what you did to him."

I had to admit... *that* was a fucking relief. But still. I wasn't going to push my luck.

"He was helping people construct false defences," I said.

Lucas nodded. "Yeah, we thought as much ourselves. Every rotten little fucker he dealt with had *some* excuse. And some of them didn't wash. Or maybe bought them enough time to do a runner. But he got a lot of those bastards off."

Lucas shook his head in despair.

"I'm sorry," I said. "I'm sorry I broke our agreement."

"Don't be," he said, looking up. "You should have done a better fucking job on him, though. I'll say that."

"Have you seen him since?"

"Once or twice," said Lucas. "But not in the nick. He never went back to work, anyway. But after things panned out the way they did here, I ain't been back either."

I didn't know what to say. It was awkward. On balance, it seemed better to let him talk.

"I saw him in the paper after the investigations were dropped. Said he was going to sue the police for some shit or other. He didn't look too fucking pretty, I can tell you. He was like one of those zombie things from the horror films. No lips."

I remembered. I'd tied Rupert to a chair and carefully stitched his lips together. When I poured the vinegar on, it must have hurt badly. His natural reaction had been to scream, and his lips had ripped against the strength of the stitching. As he screamed out, his mouth was just a blood-filled, mangled-up hole. Tattered and shredded lips, flapping loosely and pouring with blood.

He refused plastic surgery afterwards and it left him looking like something from *Hellraiser*. Pretty fucking apt, it seemed.

"They called him The Devil's Advocate," he said. "Did you know that?"

I nodded. "Yeah, I knew."

Lucas knocked back his whisky. Poured another.

There was an awkward silence as I weighed up whether to probe him for information about Claire. But once again, it seemed I didn't need to worry.

"She left me a year ago," he said. "She couldn't live with what went down here. You saved our lives and we were all really fucking grateful. But she knew something was up when I sent her upstairs that night, just after you untied us all. She heard you call that fucking psycho your mum. It didn't take her long to figure out I knew who you were and she didn't like that I covered for you. She couldn't live with the lies."

Listening to this was horrible. By the looks of it, the whole mess had driven him to drink. He was in a bad way, for sure. And it was all my fault.

"I couldn't grass you up, though. Even when you went after Bond. Considering how much I hated that bastard, it didn't seem like such a big deal. I still felt I owed you. And then you left town and there was no more Revengelist anyway."

"She wanted to go to the police? To tell them about me?"

Lucas nodded. "I told her that, by then, it was just too damn late. I mean, they might have protected her. But I scared her out of doing it by saying she'd go down for perverting, she'd take me with her, and the kids would end up in care. She just couldn't take it anymore."

Every time I learned something new, it piled on the guilt. He'd *allowed* his marriage to go tits up to cover for me. It was hard to listen to it. And it was hard seeing the wreck of a man sitting in front of me, boozed-up to fuck.

"Do you have *any* idea what happened the night she disappeared?"

"She'd gone out for her sister's hen do. Her old man sat with the kids but I didn't know that at the time. I went to her house drunk. Intending to plead with her to come back to me, but when *he* answered the door, I felt this terrible anger and jealousy. He said she'd gone out and she deserved to have some fun for a change and he told me to get back in my car and fuck off."

"What did *you* do?"

Lucas sighed with self-reproach. "I told him he'd messed with the wrong man. But I didn't do anything. I just came home and drank 'til I passed out. I was so angry and so damn jealous. She was out having fun *without* me. For all I knew she could've been out with some other bloke. She wasn't, of course. But by the time I knew that, I was in police fucking custody."

"Because of what you'd said to her dad?"

Lucas finished his cigarette and stubbed it out. He necked his drink and lit a fresh smoke.

"Exactly," he said. "It was an obvious move, but they had no evidence to charge me with anything. I hadn't *done* anything anyway! I was here, sleeping off the booze."

Lucas dragged again. He saw me looking back at him. I felt so bad for him, I just didn't know what to say.

"So, what is it I can do for you?" he said. "Have you got an idea who this Skull-Fuck bastard is? An *auntie* of yours this time? Or maybe some distant cousin?"

I shook my head, sorrowfully. "No. I don't have a clue. But I came here because of Rachel."

His eyes widened in horror. "What about Rachel?"

"Don't you know? Rachel has been taken, too. I got a note."

Lucas looked as though he'd just seen a ghost. "Show me."

I rummaged in my pocket. Dug out the note I'd been left at Gav's. "Here," I said, passing it to him. "I was due to meet her in town this morning but she didn't turn up and *this* was waiting for me."

I watched as Lucas read it, and read it again. He put it down and thumped the table. "That motherfucker!" He clamped his cigarette in his mouth, squinting against the smoke. His hand dropped to the pocket of his grubby dressing-gown and a moment later he threw a piece of paper across the table at me.

"I got one too," he said. "It was waiting for me after I was released from the nick."

I unfolded the piece of paper and read what was printed there.

I'm gonna make sure I get everything I need from this first one, and you can be sure I'll enjoy every last skull-fucking minute of it.

* * *

"How come you haven't taken it to the police?" I said.

"I did take it to the police! *That's* a photocopy I took beforehand. I wasn't gonna to have them thinking I was involved in it. Why haven't *you* taken yours to the police?"

I folded the note up and put it back in my pocket, pretty sharpish. "It's complicated," I said.

"Complicated, my arse," he growled. "You're going after him, aren't you?"

"I was going to, yes. The note I got was addressed to me personally. There was a reason for that. And there was a reason for sabotaging my meeting with Rachel."

"Why were you meeting her?"

"She asked me for my help. She said that something bad had happened. I think she was hoping –"

And *that* was when it finally dawned on me.

Lucas looked at me, waiting. But with my train of thought diverted, he must have seen on my face that something new had occurred to me.

"What is it?" he said.

"Your note. It wasn't addressed by name, was it?"

"No," said Lucas. "So what?"

"And the others? When their families got notes, were theirs addressed by name?"

"No," said Lucas. "I have a contact in the force who's been drip-feeding me bits of information. The notes were pretty much all like mine."

"Then *mine* was the only one! Whoever sent it – in fact, whoever sent them *all* – has specifically been trying to get at me the whole time. I'd bet my right nut that Rachel didn't even email me!"

"What? Why?"

"Skull-Fuck *wanted* me at that café. He tricked me into thinking I was meeting Rachel in order to get that note to me. I don't know why, but he wanted me involved in this somehow. And that means until we figure out what's going on, we're just pawns in a game and *he's* the motherfucker making up the rules."

* * *

"Listen," said Lucas. "If you think there's something big going down, we need to go to the police. Share information. This is *their* job."

"No offence, Detective, but one of the only coppers I ever trusted is sitting right in front of me drowning in a bottle of scotch, and the other has been taken by this fucking nut. I don't have a lot of faith in the rest."

Lucas looked offended, as though I'd just called his mother a whore. "Well, *no offence*, Jack, but you're not exactly so completely fucking sane yourself, and when it comes down to it, you're just *one* fucking weirdo with a leather gimp-mask who likes hurting people. What do you think *you* can do that they can't?"

I looked him straight in the eye and smiled. "I can do exactly that," I said. "I can *hurt* people."

* * *

I woke the next morning and checked the time. It was 9.30am; Lucas had gone up to bed around 2am with a gutful of whisky, so I didn't expect him to have sprung out of bed just yet.

He'd let me crash on the sofa. There was a slight chill as I padded through to his kitchen and put the kettle on. A few minutes later, there were two strong cups of coffee waiting to be drunk.

I went down the hall and stood at the bottom of the stairs. "Detective! Coffee's up!"

I waited, and heard him groaning from his bed.

"Come on," I said. "We need to get a shift on!"

I waited a bit longer and he shouted, "What fucking time is it?"

"It's nearly midday," I said. "Hurry up. The day's wasting!"

I went back to the kitchen, picked up a coffee and sat at the table. It was in this very kitchen, three years ago, that I struck my own Mum in the head with a hammer. In which she gasped my name just seconds before dying. And I cared about it for a moment. I shed a fucking *tear* for her. But I was angry with myself for that, really. Like Gran, she didn't deserve my tears. My feelings. She didn't deserve my love, because she never gave *me* any.

But this kitchen wasn't just the kitchen I killed my Mum in. It was also the kitchen in which a murderous nut-job was stopped, once and for all. It was the kitchen in which an innocent family were spared their lives at the very last moment. Before my mother smashed their skulls in one by one and removed their teeth for souvenirs.

Ultimately, despite the death, it was a place where something very good had happened. And I was the one who had done that good.

But just how good had it all turned out to be?

I had placed the family in a position where they felt obliged to lie for me. And when it became a problem for his personal life, Lucas remained immovable in his dedication to stay tight-lipped. But because of that, he'd lost his whole damn family.

So how much good did I really do? How much good could I do *now*?

I didn't know. It was probably all a matter of perception. Because when I finally found Skull-Fuck I was going to make him pay. No two ways about *that*. And although it might be frowned upon by the law, plenty of people would thank me for it.

That, I knew from experience.

* * *

Lucas came thudding down the stairs about ten minutes later.

"My fucking head hurts," he said. "Where's that coffee?"

I pointed it out to him. As he went to the side to collect it, he must have seen the clock on the microwave.

"I thought you said it was nearly midday," he said.

"I lied."

He came and sat down. Sipped his coffee. "I feel like something Death crapped out."

I nodded at the bottle of whisky. There was about an inch left in the bottom of it. "Hair of the dog?"

He shuddered in response. "Don't even go there. Just tell me the plan."

"There's no plan," I said. "My idea was to look at the facts. To brainstorm. Try to figure something out. I thought that with you being a copper, it's the sort of thing you'd be good at."

Lucas frowned back. "Don't hold your breath," he said. "I'm not likely to be much good for an hour or two."

I stood up. Walked to the kettle and flicked the switch. "Then let's get some more coffee into you."

* * *

I scanned the notes from Skull-Fuck and put them down.

"I can't help but feel a strong sense of purpose here." I said. "Claire and Rachel make the chances of coincidence too remote for my liking."

Lucas nodded. "I agree," he said. "I think this bastard is trying to mess with your head."

"What do we know about the victims? Is there anything that *connects* them?"

"Like what, exactly?" said Lucas, frowning. "Were they all in the same knitting club? I seriously fucking doubt it. Is Skull-Fuck a mutual ex-boyfriend? I doubt that, too."

"What about your friend on the investigation? Hasn't he said anything?"

"This is no game, Jack. I'm off on extended sick leave. He's up to his arse in missing women and one of them is my ex-wife. It's the worst serial offender situation since your mother went nuts with a rusty hammer. He'll keep me posted here and there, but he won't risk fucking *anything* up just because of me."

"All right," I said. "Then we'll do some digging around of our own. *Never* underestimate the powers of the internet."

* * *

So, Claire was Lucas's ex-wife, we already knew *that*. She was a part-time volunteer for a local charity shop and a part-time secretary in a GP surgery. The two boys lived with her. Sam and Ryan, now aged fifteen and eleven. Her dad was a retired lorry driver and her mother was a member of the Salvation Army.

All very exciting.

Some of Skull-Fuck's other victims I managed to trace on Facebook, LinkedIn and Google. Certainly, to some degree, anyway.

Lisa Daniels was a nineteen-year-old art and design student with what appeared to be a large circle of friends mostly made up of musicians and poetic hippies. She liked socialising with her friends in pubs and watching them perform at open-mike nights. She liked the successful TV horror-drama *The Walking Dead* and TV comedians Russell Brand and Ricky Gervais. Her status updates were mostly kept hidden so her thoughts and opinions weren't so easy to trace. She didn't seem a particularly controversial character, though. She'd gone missing one night the month before on her way to meet her on/off boyfriend, Marcus Dowlish.

Andrea Freeman was a salaried partner with Hardwin and Barlow Solicitors. She practised employment law for private paying clients with work-based grievances. On Facebook, there were some photos of her enjoying a glass of wine or two at home with a big smile, some expensive-looking jewellery and a handsome, well-groomed husband. It seemed that in her spare time, she self-published some fairly tame erotic novels under the unenthusiastically hidden pseudonym Davina Delicia. Some of the titles included *Debriefing Chloe, Barely Legal* and *Oh God Yes, Your Honour.*

Yvonne Long was a stay-at-home housewife. She had three kids, and her husband appeared to be a car-salesman. She liked sunbeds and nail bars and thought that Jeremy Clarkson could rev *her* engine anytime he wanted. She was generally Tory in outlook, but thought that David Cameron was a complete fool. She also liked poodles dyed pink.

Tanya Maynard was a twenty-six-year-old checkout girl at Morrison's. She had a three-year-old son called Tyler and a husband called Tyson, who was not only the kindest man you'd ever hope to meet, he was also in prison after being 'stitched up' for a mugging 'he didn't do.' She enjoyed a good drink by the looks of it, and large, gold, hoop-earrings. She also advocated the occasional use of cannabis for her bad back because it didn't *always* lead to harder drugs like they always went on about. She said she knew smack-heads who'd never even touched weed. Recently, she'd been the lucky recipient of a one thousand pound pay-out from a claim against her bank for mis-sold PPI.

Olivia Graham was the only one I couldn't get much info on. I knew she worked for an advertising company called Fenwick Lambert's but she didn't have much of an online presence so there was very little I could dig up on her.

In the end, my efforts were unrewarded, and it was disappointing. I *had* hoped that I might discover something really cool. Olivia might have helped Hardwin Barlow Solicitors with a local advertising campaign, and Andrea Freeman from Hardwin Barlow might have represented Tanya Maynard in an employment dispute, and Tanya Maynard's husband might have gone inside for mugging Yvonne Long, and Yvonne Long's husband might have sold a car to Lisa Daniels, and Lisa Daniels might have been a patient at the GP surgery where Claire Edwards worked, and Rachel might have been the copper who nabbed Tyson.

But no. Nothing like that.

After all that, the only thing I found that connected each of these women was gender. That was it. I was completely and utterly stumped.

* * *

Lucas leaned over my shoulder and looked at the monitor. "Any joy?"

"Nothing," I said. "I can't find a single fucking thing that links these women."

"Go back to the Google homepage," he said. "I just want to try something."

I rolled the cursor over the Google button and sent us back to the homepage. Dropped the cursor into the search-bar and waited.

"Okay," he said. "Bring up Olivia."

I went to the drop-down search-history arrow, right on the end of the search-bar. Olivia was at the top of the search-history list, with the other names heading downwards in reverse. As I rolled the cursor towards Olivia Graham, Lucas suddenly shouted at me.

"Stop! Jack, stop!"

"What is it?"

He pointed at the screen. "It's there," he said. "Holy shit, it's actually *there!*"

* * *

I didn't have a fucking clue what he was talking about. He was pointing at the screen, at the drop-down search-history.

"There!" he said. "For Christ's sake, *there!*"

I frowned. "You're going to have to spell it out to me, I don't get it."

Lucas turned away and started rummaging for something. "It can't be a coincidence. It can't be!"

He came back with a notebook and pen. "Look," he said. Then he started writing something.

I looked down at the notebook. And this is what he wrote:

Claire
Lisa
Andrea
Yvonne
Tanya
Olivia

He looked up at me excitedly, then back down at the pad. "See it yet?"

I tried. I stared hard at the notebook but honestly, I couldn't figure out what Lucas could see.

"Er… no, I don't."

He huffed loudly. "For God's sake, Jack!" The he went back to the pad, and a moment later he thumped the page with his fist. "*Now* look."

When he moved, this is what I saw.

[C] laire
[L] isa
[A] ndrea
[Y] vonne
[T] anya
[O] livia

I saw it now, all right.

* * *

"It can't be," I said. "Rachel is the last one, to date, but an 'R' in *that* sequence wouldn't spell *anything*."

Lucas rubbed thoughtfully at several days' worth of stubble. "That would be true if Rachel was actually her first name, but it isn't."

And for a moment, an image flashed across my mind. It was my email inbox. I saw the email from Rachel, highlighted by my cursor. The email address of the sender floating before my eyes.

RACHEL N. SLATER.

"So, what *is* her first name?" I said, with a weird sense of dread.

"Nicola," he answered. "But she flipped them over. She never really liked Nicola so she went by Rachel instead."

I looked back at the notebook. I picked up Lucas's pen and finished his list.

[C] laire
[L] isa
[A] ndrea
[Y] vonne
[T] anya
[O] livia
[N] icola

I was suddenly filled with so much dread it made me sick to the stomach. We sat there in silence for a moment, and my mind raced with memories. Making connections. Coming to realisations.

* * *

It was Tuesday 12th October, and now almost three years to the day. The day that Johnny Clayton broke into Harry's house, put his grubby hands on Harry's daughter and cracked Harry over the head with his own baseball bat.

As a result of what that bastard had done, Harry had died. And it was true that he'd been hiding a heart condition. It was true that he was more likely to have a heart attack than a coked-up judge on his honeymoon night, but it had *still* been Johnny Clayton's fault.

But Johnny was dead, and the name Clayton could only mean one thing. Just thinking about it made me angry. The *nerve* of it! The sheer, bare-faced cheek of the rotten fucker.

Skull-Fuck was Bradley Clayton.

Nineteen

Lucas was looking at me with the expression of a man just slapped in the face with a wet fish.

"You know who this is, don't you?"

I looked back at him. Mine was the expression of guilt. "I think so," I said, turning back to the computer screen.

Lucas waited for a moment and then encouraged me to continue with a rough nudge to the shoulder. "Cough it up!" he said.

I tapped in a Google search for any kind of news report concerning my old colleague, Harry. Before long, we were looking at an article from three years ago. The report of Harry's break-in, leading to the heart attack which hospitalised him.

"This," I said to Lucas, "was a guy I worked with. He was one of the good guys. You might remember him."

Lucas nodded. "Yeah. Harry McKinley, right?"

"That's right," I said. "An old client of mine by the name of Johnny Clayton was arrested, based on description, for breaking into Harry's house, bashing Harry over the head with a baseball bat, touching up his fifteen-year-old daughter and stealing some jewellery. The first heart attack he suffered put him in a hospital bed. The second one put him in a grave."

"I remember!" said Lucas. "Clayton was represented by Rupert fucking Bond, and he came up with some bullshit alibi, so we had to release him."

I nodded. A moment or two passed, in which other connections were made.

He looked at me. Eyes widening. "Clayton was found dead a couple of days later! It was you, wasn't it?"

I nodded again. "When I went to his house, it was to punish him for the burglary and for fiddling with Harry's kid. But whilst I was there, I learned that Harry had suffered his fatal heart attack and I fucking lost it. Before I finished with Johnny, though, his brother turned up and came at me with a baseball bat. I got Johnny Clayton; that was inevitable. But I think all *this* – this Skull-Fuck shit – is Bradley Clayton. I think he's gunning for me. Trying to get my attention. That's why he went after Rachel."

"Shit! Bradley reported the attack on his brother but we weren't convinced we were dealing with The Revengelist because you normally left that fucking business card."

"Yeah, I had to make a pretty hasty exit," I said.

Lucas paused.

"He wasn't taken seriously. Another dead junkie, so fucking what? The police didn't care. They thought it was probably drugs-related. But why Claire?" he said. "Why did he go after *her*?"

I looked back gravely. "Because she had information," I said. "She knew who *I* was."

* * *

I saw it. I saw the look he gave me as I said that, and it was unmistakable. A quick and accusatory flash. An instinctive reaction, I knew that, and part of me could forgive him for it. But still. I was now in the company of a man who knew that I was to blame for his ex-wife *and* ex-colleague going missing and quite possibly being hurt by some nick-named psycho with revenge on his mind.

He knew it. Just as he knew that covering for me had driven his wife out the front door.

There might only be so long he was willing to play best buddies. Only so long he was willing to offer me smiles instead of hate-filled grimacing. I knew I was on thin ice, and the *I Saved Your Life* card was losing its sway.

I had to tread carefully from now on. The ice was getting thinner all the time.

* * *

"We need some sort of plan," said Lucas, sweeping his hair back.

Those tired and hung-over eyes from earlier, all red and bloodshot. His mind, filled with a thousand visions he didn't want to see, but couldn't turn off.

Visions, probably, of Claire in her vulnerable state. Tied up by some psycho-freak motherfucker-

(In pain?)

(Bleeding, maybe?)

- and completely helpless. I wouldn't have believed him if he denied it. I was having them too.

"Yes," I said. "We need a plan, but I've got nothing. You?"

Lucas smiled. "I still have a few tricks up my sleeve," he said.

* * *

Lucas was in another room, on the phone to his mate in the force. My paranoia about this was having an almighty freak-out. I was tempted to slip out of Lucas's house and make a run for it. Part of me was absolutely convinced he was grassing me up.

But I stuck it out. I strained as hard as I could to hear his muffled voice. His bass frequencies, reverberating through the thin walls. But actual words?

No joy.

In time, he came back into the study with a big grin on his face.

"Fucking bingo!" he said.

* * *

Lucas's mate had remembered Bradley Clayton, too. I wasn't sure how, but Lucas had managed to talk him into giving up Clayton's home address.

Truthfully? I was doubtful. Lucas himself had said that his mate would drip-feed information here and there but wouldn't risk fucking up the investigation. How had he managed to sweet-talk this man into giving out *that* kind of detail?

Lucas was probably stitching me up, and sooner or later I'd come undone. It was likely that he was trading information about me to get the information he needed to help rescue Claire.

I was sure of it.

But for now, it looked like we needed each other. Lucas had access to resources I did not. We'd already made progress by banging our heads together. But for Lucas, I was probably the bargaining chip. He might not get much further without having me on hand to apply a bit of squeeze here and there, and when the shit finally hit the fan he could use me with a nicely timed shove in the back and a good dose of, "Here's what you're after, now release my ex-wife!"

I just had to try to keep my eyes peeled. Stay alert to any warning signs that things were suddenly going to turn a little back-stabby.

* * *

Lucas and I were in the Mustang. I was suited up and the old Revengelist clobber felt good, to tell the truth. Tight and tough. I felt that menacing vibe all over again, like a mean motherfucker, and it was good.

Lucas sat beside me in the passenger seat. "Nice fucking car," he said.

"Cheers," I said, leaning heavier on the accelerator. Showing off a bit.

The engine roared like a lion and the car picked up speed. I felt like Tim Burton's *Batman*. Sinister and enigmatic. That scene when he's heading back to the Bat Cave with Vicki Vale in the next seat; when she's desperately trying to glimpse the man beneath the mask. It didn't matter that Lucas knew who I was. I still felt pretty cool at that moment.

Soon enough, we were in the shit-hole parts of town. Bradley's address was another ramshackle dump in a red-brick estate. We cruised around for a while and eventually found it among the turny-twisty maze of identical streets. A scraggy and unkempt garden out front. Some pound-shop Christmas lights that hadn't been taken down from last year. A grubby and sagging England flag hanging in a bedroom window.

Lucas was looking over the road and I nodded to confirm.

"That's our house," I said.

"It looks empty."

I agreed. It had an abandoned look to it. Did the council think Bradley still lived here?

We should have dug deeper. We could have made some enquiries and established whether he was still living here. But it was the same old story. Should have, could have, would have. You never think until it's too late.

We were now sitting outside and it was 10pm and it was dark and I didn't want to waste any more time. We didn't have time to waste.

"How do you think we ought to handle this?" said Lucas. Breaking into houses was not his thing. Not without a warrant and a team of highly-trained armed coppers, anyway.

I nodded to the alleyway further down the road. "I always find the back way accommodating," I said.

* * *

Bradley's back garden was even messier than the front. The clues were clear, I thought. The house had been abandoned for a while; it looked neglected.

Part of me had a very bad feeling.

Lucas shuffled up behind me as I approached the back door. I took hold of the handle and...

Unlocked!

But *why* was it unlocked? Was Clayton setting us up? I didn't like this.

"Are we in?" whispered Lucas.

I nodded. "We're in," I said.

* * *

It was different to snooping around Rachel's house. It was still eerie. There was still a sense of dread, but it was for different reasons. In Rachel's house, it felt like trespass. Plus, I was worried about finding her dead. Here, I didn't know what the hell I might find. And I didn't feel like an intruder. I was eager to find Bradley Clayton and hurt him. I also felt a sense of unfairness that the situation had put *me* on the back foot. That I was the one stepping through hoops; hoops he *wanted* me to step through. One at a time, like a performing monkey.

We stepped through the kitchen at the back of the house. Down the hall to the lounge/diner and so far there was nothing. The place was a disgusting mess. It stank of something I didn't even want to think about. Like spoiled meat.

There was something claustrophobic about the place, too. It was dark and gloomy, and not just because it was a late-autumn night. The dirty curtains were drawn, and there was a close, tense vibe. Even through my leathers, I felt grimy and grubby. Breathing the air in here made me feel like dirt was entering my body. Infiltrating and infecting me. I could visualise the muck and filth going in, depositing in my lungs. I could visualise extreme close-up pictures of bacteria squirming around and multiplying, just like you see on TV science programs.

I thought I was going to puke.

"There's nothing down here," said Lucas. "Do you want to head upstairs?"

I didn't. I *really* didn't. I felt horrible. All swimmy in the head, and queasy in the guts. But I knew we had to.

"Come on," I said.

And led the way.

* * *

Bedroom one was empty. Bedroom two had a few neatly stacked boxes in it, but nothing else. As we stepped out, back on to the landing, a sort of sinking feeling filled my guts. A disappointment. I'd managed to get my hopes up that coming here would be helpful. That we might find something to spur us on. A clue. A message, even.

It was beginning to look as though psychos just weren't as dependable as you'd hope.

I watched Lucas move through to the master bedroom and waited on the landing, hands on the stair-well banister, wallowing in self-pity and disappointment. Thinking about where we'd go next. And that was when Lucas croaked nervously from the bedroom.

"Jack?"

It was in the tone of his voice. I knew it.

Fucking bingo!

* * *

I stepped through and it hit me immediately. The smell of spoiled meat when we entered the house. The source was in *here*.

A street-light glow from outside gently illuminated the horrors all around us. So many things hit me, all at the same time, and I just didn't know how to make sense of it all.

The walls were stripped of wallpaper and divided into sections by thickly drawn chalk lines. There were seven sections in all, each one marked with a huge chalk letter, moving around the room from the door-frame in a clockwise direction.

The letters spelled out 'CLAYTON'.

Within each of the divisions, Bradley had stuck various Polaroids, surrounding the big chalk letters; radiating outwards on wobbly, chalk-drawn spokes, like a child's bubble-diagram. In section C, the Polaroids were all of Claire Edwards. In section L, they were of Lisa Daniels, and so on like this, all the way round.

The pictures appeared to be organised with a loose degree of chronology, so that the ones closer to the letter at the centre were the ones taken immediately after their abduction.

Each woman wore the look of terror and confusion. Each photo, the close-up, over-exposure of a sudden flash-bulb in the dark. And as they moved away from the chalk letter, each picture told the tale of their torment. The tired, haggard faces. The dirty clothes. The decreasing terror and the grim acceptance.

This room was a gallery of human suffering.

But the smell of spoiled meat? Well, *that* was coming from a small table in the centre of the room. There was no other furniture in here. The room was completely bare, with stripped walls and stripped floors.

But in the centre, that table. And placed upon the table was a large, severed pig's head that appeared to have gone badly off. One of its dead and lifeless eyes was still there. The other was not. It had been scooped out, and the empty eye-socket was now stuffed with a huge rubber cock.

The pig's head had been skull-fucked.

* * *

"Oh, God," said Lucas. He moved over to the section of wall marked C, drawn inextricably by the terrible images. "Oh, Jesus fucking Christ!"

He reached up a hand and lightly traced his fingers over the photos. The pictures of his ex-wife's face. Caught crying. Caught screaming. Caught pleading. And as the pictures moved away from the centre, he could see the terror in her eyes give way to a soul-crushing acquiescence. A haunting and submissive compliance. I could see it in her eyes, and so could Lucas. She'd basically accepted that she was going to die in whatever shit-hole Bradley was keeping her and it was all over her face.

It was pretty much the same for the other victims, too. It was depressing. It was utterly depressing.

Lucas turned to me. "We've got to catch this motherfucker, Jack," he said, in a soft, flat tone. "We gotta catch him as soon as possible."

"I know," I said. I was looking at the pig. Something had caught my eye. "We'll get him."

I walked over to the little table. And I could see it now. Something papery, wedged into the pig's half-open mouth. I bent down, level with the stinking thing. Peered into its mouth. Reached up a hand. Poked my fingers in and extracted the piece of paper.

I stood, and looked it over.

It was a rectangular piece of paper, like a compliment slip. On one side, was a message to me.

It said:

Jack Jones
You are hereby summoned to stand trial on charges of:
Assault, Burglary, Torture, Murder,
And interfering in shit that don't concern you.
Venue: The Old Courthouse.

At the bottom, was this:

And on the other side:

R.B. Property Management
October Statement – Mr B. Clayton
Rent Due: £00.00

"What *is* that?" said Lucas. His voice came to me through the muffling wall of shock I suddenly felt. Watery and distant. "Jack, what is it?"

I snapped back to it. "This is what we've been looking for," I said distractedly.

Lucas snatched it from my hands. "Let me look!" he said. He examined it. Flipped it over impatiently, and back again. "What the fuck does *that* mean?" he said.

"I guess we're going to find out."

I glanced around the squalid room for some hint of another clue but there was nothing. We'd found all there was to find.

"Let's get the fuck out of here," said Lucas.

Twenty

The Old Courthouse that Skull-Fuck was referring to in his summons was exactly that.

It was a former magistrates' court. A beautifully Gothic, Victorian building that fell into disrepair a long time ago. I didn't know a great deal about the place but rumour had it the last hangings took place over a hundred years ago. Thieves, murderers, whatever. It made no difference, and neither did age. Several children got the rope there, too.

It was fair to say that I had some strong views on justice. Lord knows, some nasty bastards had paid for the things they'd done at my hands, and they'd fucking deserved it. But hanging children? That was just fucking wrong.

The human race has demonstrated throughout history that its belief about civilised culture is essentially based upon a great big fucking lie. A self-deception. Large-scale delusions of grandeur. Humanity has a lot to be ashamed of, and I don't see it learning much from its mistakes for a very long time. This Old Courthouse, to me, was just another example of that. Proof of the bullshit we tell ourselves. Proof of our tendency to disown, forsake, bury and hide. To sweep the dust beneath the rug. Because when the truth hurts, let it wither. Let it be disowned, forsaken, buried and hidden.

The Old Courthouse was a beautiful piece of architecture. It truly was. But it was all that was beautiful about it. Just like Mum and Frank's house, the Old Courthouse was a vault of pain, death, injustice and Big overpowering Small.

Powerful over helpless. Small-mindedness. Corruption. Ignorance. And General Human Rottenness.

All the things I hated. And just because it was being done in the name of justice, it didn't make it right.

Does that make me sound like a fucking hypocrite?

I don't care. Fuck you. The things I've done have not been motivated by corruption, ignorance or stupidity. Nor through sadism for sadism's sake, or general human rottenness. The things I've done have been motivated by the fact that our country is run by a bunch of greedy, self-interested twats.

Whether ignorance and corruption are *enforcing* the law, or *flouting* it, you can bet your arse on one thing. I fucking hate it. Which is why I hated everything that the Old Courthouse stood for.

* * *

Some wealthy toff developer had snapped the place up a few years ago. Word was, the place was going to be renovated and turned into flats. But for some reason, the plans dried up and didn't go anywhere. Despite being boarded up, the occasional squatter or drunken homeless bum had made a temporary home in it. Littering the space inside with empty beer cans and druggy shit. Food wrappers. Used johnnies.

The place probably stank to high heaven of piss.

The whole thing was a stain; a smear on life, of all that was wrong with humanity, and it needed knocking down. And *this* was where Skull-Fuck wanted me to go? This was where he wanted to finish the game?

I guess it all made sense, really.

* * *

Lucas and I were sitting in the Mustang. My hands were gripping the steering-wheel. His were clenched into fists and resting on his thighs. We were both staring ahead, out of the windscreen. But neither of us was looking at anything in particular.

Lucas was the first to speak.

"We need to tool up," he said. "I'm not going into this without some serious fucking hardware."

Still staring ahead, I nodded. "What are we talking about here? Guns?"

But I *knew* he wasn't talking about sharp sticks.

"Well, we're *not* talking about knives. Remember *The Untouchables*? Don't bring a knife to a gunfight? *That* is what I'm talking about."

I turned and looked at him. Inside, I was blazing and raging with hate and anger. On the outside, I was as cool and calm as I could be.

"I don't do guns," I said.

Lucas nodded. "Well, don't mind me when I say fuck that. We'll head back to mine first. We'll pick up what we need and then we're going to finish this. Okay?"

I started the engine. Shoved it into gear. Pumped the accelerator.

"Sounds like a plan," I said, and off we went.

* * *

Think of any action movie. Think of a scene where the hero, just before the final showdown, gets himself suited up. Think of rapidly-edited sequences where guns are loaded. Stuffed angrily into holsters and all available pockets. Think of black fingerless gloves yanked on; hands flexing into fists and back. Think of black war-paint smeared onto cheeks, tough-guy grimaces and Lock and Load. Think of battle-ready music. Drums thumping and pounding and deadly-serious strings which let you know the hero's had enough and Means Fucking Business.

Well, *this* was nothing like that.

We pulled up outside Lucas's house and went in. He chucked his keys on the kitchen table and combed his fingers through his sweaty hair.

"Right," he said. "Gun!"

He strode from the room and went upstairs. As I waited, I opened a few of his kitchen drawers, looking for a knife. I didn't want something rubbish. I wanted something proper psychotic, like Michael Myers. I found a drawer with a medium-sized ceramic vegetable knife, and thought about it. Then I grabbed it up and stashed it in my vest and carried on looking.

In the end I found what I was looking for. I noticed that the light reflecting off the kitchen window made a mirror. Standing there in all my Revengelist stuff, I posed for myself and admired my reflection. Light glinting off the huge blade in my hand.

Mean, I thought. *A proper mean motherfucker!*

A moment later, Lucas came thudding down the stairs. He had a handgun-case which was padlocked. He came into the kitchen and threw the case on the table in frustration.

"I can't find the fucking key," he said.

"Well, where did you have it last?"

Lucas rolled his eyes. "If I knew that, then it wouldn't be fucking lost, would it?"

In the end, we hack-sawed it open.

* * *

Okay; so, huge, proper-psycho kitchen knife?

Check.

Smaller, ceramic knife?

Check.

Lucas, with his gun?

Check.

Balls of steel?

Of course, fucking check!

So, I looked at Lucas. "You ready?"

He patted the pocket where his handgun was stashed. "Fucking ready," he said.

I nodded. I had a really bad feeling all of a sudden. I wasn't going to chicken out. Not now. But looking at the big sign on the fence around the Old Courthouse gave me cause for a very deep concern indeed.

The building belonged to R. B. Property Management.

"All right then," I said. "Let's do this."

* * *

I went in first. We scaled the chain-link fence and moved stealthily across a weedy, scraggy plot of land. Keeping low. Keeping quiet.

Sticking with the principle that the back way was always the easiest, we crept around the building to the rear. I tested a couple of the ground-level windows and found one that slid up with ease. The room it opened into looked like it might have once been some sort of clerk's office. But now it was just a shit-hole. Beer bottles and cider cans. Pizza boxes and graffiti. Needles. The butt-ends of joints smoked long ago.

I looked at Lucas. "If you hold it open, I'll go through first," I whispered.

He nodded. Took hold of the window and held it open as I clambered in and lowered myself into the building.

"What a fucking dump!" I hissed.

"Come on," said Lucas. "Take the window."

I supported the sash as he climbed in. As he set himself down, I started to lower it again, and then thought better of it.

"Lucas, pass me that, will you?"

Lucas picked up the empty beer can I wanted. Passed it to me. I jammed it into the sash-runner to keep the window from falling. I turned and saw that Lucas was looking at me.

"For a quick getaway," I said.

He nodded. "You *have* done this before, haven't you?"

"Come on," I said, and led the way.

We stepped out of the office and carefully through a dark and pissy hallway. In the half-light I saw some interesting graffiti.

No such thing as crime. No such thing as justice.
There's only action and revenge.

Too fucking right, I thought, and moved off down the hall, creeping cautiously. Within a moment or so we came to a large door that was standing ajar.

"I think this might be it," I whispered to Lucas, pointing to his pocket. "Be ready."

Lucas just nodded once. Grim and resolute.

I reached out. My gloved hands on the surface of the door. But would it creak and signal our arrival? Was anyone in the next room, waiting for me? Was this me walking into an ambush?

There was only one way to find out.

I pushed the door open. The disused courtroom beyond was lit with a few randomly placed candles, flickering gently in the late-night gloom. I stepped in and looked around. Senses on red alert. I sensed Lucas shuffle up close behind me and then I heard it.

The booming voice.

"Come in, Jack!"

I looked to the back of the room. The old magistrates' bench had been ripped out years ago. All the furniture was long gone. It was just an empty chamber, aglow with the light of a few candles.

But I could now see a large and well-built man standing with his hands linked in front of him. The pose of a security guard. Black trousers, black jacket. A white skull-mask with a big red F stamped on the forehead. Trickles of blood from empty eye-sockets.

It was Skull-Fuck. It was Bradley fucking Clayton.

And *that* was exactly when the world went black.

* * *

I had absolutely no idea how long I was out. When I came to, I was aware of a number of things.

My hat and mask had been removed. I was standing on a rickety old wooden chair. Skull-Fuck and Rodney Lucas were looking up at me. My hands were bound behind me and there was a rope noose around my neck.

I looked at Lucas. "Was that *you* that fucking hit me?"

Lucas had a sheepish look about him. Something was happening here, and I had a fair idea what it was.

"I'm sorry, Jack," he said. "I didn't have a choice."

"You're handing me over to save the women, aren't you?"

His eyes said it all. There was the vaguest nod of his head, but his eyes were apologetic and pleading with me to understand. I could see that. He had given me up to save his ex-wife. His friend. All the others.

I *could* understand that. He'd covered for me for long enough.

"I'm sorry." It was all he could say.

"All right!" said Skull-Fuck. Through the mask, I recognised the voice -

(I'm gonna smash your fucking skull in!)

- from three years before. The confrontation in Johnny's front room. Right before I killed him and jumped out the window. The last thing I saw was Bradley, hurling his baseball bat after me and screaming into the night.

The skull-mask tilted. Bradley was looking up at me.

"Jack Jones, you have been summoned here to answer charges of assault, burglary, torture and murder. And just generally being a complete prick. How do you plead?"

"Fuck you," I said. "Where's Rachel? Where are the other women, you psycho fuck?"

"Ha!" he yelled. "Look who's talking! I *asked* you how you plead."

"And I said 'fuck you'!"

Bradley raised his hands, as though he had a gathering of spectators. Like some show-off hot-shot lawyer in an American TV legal drama, playing to an audience.

"The Court will accept 'fuck you' as a plea of not guilty! Please let the records show that the defendant is non-compliant and hostile, and to give this due consideration when he is found guilty."

I looked at Lucas. Again, that look was on his face. Anxious and uncertain. Like he wasn't sure where this was going either.

"Okay!" said Bradley. "Now if the Court will please be upstanding for the trial judge in this matter –"

He looked over at me. Then at Lucas. And he nodded to himself, satisfied.

"Introducing, His Honour Judge Bond!"

And that was when things fell into place, and when sense was made of some outstanding questions I had, and when I felt my guts roll sickeningly in on themselves.

The man who stepped through a side-door near Bradley Clayton was, of course, the severely disfigured Devil's Advocate, Rupert Bond.

Twenty One

Conjure up an image in your mind. Think of the *Hellraiser* movies of the eighties. Think of the 'Chatterer Cenobite'. Its mouth all lipless and peeled back. Teeth and gums exposed.

That was what Rupert Bond looked like. Hideously deformed. Piercing eyes, bright and alert. The permanent ugly grin of madness. He was wearing a black robe and a judge's horse-hair wig.

In a momentary flash of insight, I put two and two together. I saw in my mind's eye the scrap of paper that the summons was written on. The rent statement from *R.B. Property Management.* The same company that owned this run-down shit-hole.

R. B. Property Management.

Rupert Bond.

It was *Rupert* who owned the Old Courthouse, and he'd clearly bought Bradley's house from the council, keeping Bradley there rent-free in exchange for his help with the physical stuff. The Dirty Work.

The plan had probably been Bond's. Bradley was just the hired-goon.

And something else made sense, too. It was Lucas's phone call. The one I couldn't make out all too well, from the next room. He hadn't been speaking to some mate in the force at all. He'd been speaking to Bradley. Finding out what to do and where to go next.

Fuck it!

He'd been in on the thing, in so far as a metaphorical gun was being held to his head. Claire had been kidnapped and Lucas had been a suspect. It was obvious he had nothing to do with the actual kidnapping, but at some point or other he'd been roped into luring me here. Presumably believing that Bond would release his ex-wife. And hopefully Rachel.

I'd been sucked in. Played like a total mug.

But there was one thing I knew that *none* of these fuckers did. One thing I had going for me that they hadn't counted on.

They didn't know that I couldn't feel pain.

* * *

He came into the courtroom chamber and sat himself down in another rickety-looking chair, much like the one that stood between me and a death by hanging.

Bradley went and stood beside him, as loyal as a lap-dog. Lucas looked at me, uncertainly. Worry in his eyes.

"Hello, Jack," said Bond. "What an awful predicament you've found yourself in, eh?"

That was what he said. What it sounded like when *he* spoke it though, was: *Hello, Jack. What'n awshul gredicanent you'sh hound yourshelsh in, eh?*

"Yes," I said. "Although not quite as bad as that speech impediment."

"Yes, very funny," he said. (*Yesh, sherry shunny.*) "But you won't be laughing when I find you guilty. You'll be dying."

"What about the women? Are you going to release them?"

Rupert's eyes twinkled. Given that he couldn't smile, I guessed that this was him finding something humorous. "Well, that all depends," he said.

Lucas flinched.

"It depends on what?" I said.

"On the verdict, of course!"

He seemed to find something very funny indeed. His laugh sounded like someone with bronchitis, coughing up their guts.

Lucas stepped forward. "You promised me you'd release them. You promised me that if I delivered Jack, you'd release them all!"

Bradley stepped forward, too. It was defensive in nature. Protecting Rupert, by the looks of it.

"Yeah, well," he said. "Like Darth Vader said: we've changed the terms of the deal. Pray we don't change them any further."

"What the fuck's that meant to mean?"

"It means," said Rupert, "that you have one more duty to perform. This Court needs a prosecutor to present the case against the defendant."

* * *

This was just getting better by the minute.

I didn't have long, and I knew it. Behind my back, I wriggled my wrists as discretely as I could. The rope had been tied tight. But these guys were clearly not sea-faring, knot-tying bastards. With enough wriggling and enough lubrication, I could probably do a Harry Houdini before they kicked the chair out from beneath my feet.

The only lubrication I could get *here*, of course, was my own blood. And that was why it was just as well I felt no pain.

"Wait!" I said. "Does that mean I get representation too?"

"Ah ha!" said Bond. "You're one step ahead of me, Jack. Of course, you get representation. This is, after all, a civilised society in which we live, is it not?"

He then turned to Bradley. "Bring her out," he said.

Bradley walked out the door through which Bond had entered. A few moments later, he was dragging a woman back through. Her hands were bound behind her. Her legs thrashing around. She was whimpering through a taped-up mouth and her clothes were grubby and blood-spotted. When Bradley stood her up and spun her round to face me, her eyes bulged in horror.

It was Rachel.

* * *

Bradley ripped the tape off her face and she let out a cry.

"Jack!" she yelled.

I tried to smile reassuringly. I don't think I pulled it off. "I'm all right," I said. "It's going to be all right."

"Okay!" boomed Rupert. "My assistant here will explain how this will work. Mr Clayton?"

Bradley stepped forward. His skull-mask moved from left to right, surveying us all.

Lucas, who was looking tired. And haggard. And thoroughly pissed off.

Rachel, who also looked tired. And dirty. And terror-stricken.

Me, not far from being hung by the neck until dead.

"Okay," he said. "This is what's going to happen. His Honour Judge Bond is here to preside over the trial of *this* piece of shit." He was pointing to me. "But any cunting around, and we'll just hang him without warning. Mr Lucas, you are the prosecution and it is your job to prove that Jack is guilty. Miss Slater, you're

Jack's defence. It is your rather hopeless task to prove that Jack here is *not* guilty. The allegations we will be trying tonight are allegations of burglary, torture and assault of Mr Reginald Chesterfield. Burglary, torture and assault of Mr Mick Miller. And last but not least, burglary, torture and *murder* of my brother, Mr Johnny Clayton. In order to assist us in these proceedings, Mr Bond has prepared the prosecution case for you, Mr Lucas."

Bradley reached into his coat pocket and produced a bundle of papers stapled together in the top left-hand corner. He leaned forward and passed them to Lucas.

"And for you, Miss Slater... the best of luck. You're going to need it because I can tell you now, you probably don't stand much chance."

Rachel looked up at me. There was guilt in her eyes. A *pre-emptive* guilt. She fully understood what was happening here, and she knew she stood no chance of persuading them that I wasn't guilty. The whole thing was a game. We all knew that no matter what happened here, I was going to die. This whole bullshit façade was like a cat toying with a mouse before ripping its head off.

"Oh," said Bradley. "And one other thing. Mr Lucas; should you persuade His Honour that Jack is guilty of the offences he stands charged with, the women will be released. Miss Slater; if you should be lucky enough to persuade His Honour that Jack is innocent, the women, unfortunately, are going to die."

Rachel burst into tears. It was the most haunting and depressing sound ever. It was awful. I'd never heard anything so defeated and so miserable in all my life.

This whole thing was probably the biggest stitch-up in the history of rotten fucking stitch-ups.

* * *

Lucas shook the pages. Straightened them out and held them in front of him, as though preparing to make a wedding speech. Then he cleared his throat.

"This is the case against the defendant," he said. His voice had the quivering quality of a complete lack of conviction.

Bond rubbed his hands together excitedly. I would have said he was grinning, but he could hardly turn that ugly fucking smile off now, could he?

"Jack Jones," said Lucas, waving in my general direction, "was a criminal defence paralegal for Robert Mitchell, solicitors. He used 'inside' knowledge to target his clients in a completely unjustified and unlawful series of vigilante attacks. His first victim was department store Father Christmas, Mr Reginald Chesterfield – a seventy-five-year-old widower awaiting trial in relation to several charges of possessing indecent images of children."

He paused. He knew what was coming next.

We all did.

"On the evening of Friday the fifth of October, three years ago, the defendant broke into Mr Chesterfield's home address, tied him up and gagged him, then proceeded to barbarically remove Mr Chesterfield's penis with a pair of garden secateurs."

"*Guilty!*" Bond suddenly screeched.

Bradley placed a hand on Bond's shoulder. "Not just yet, Your Honour. Not just yet."

It had the very obvious vibe of a scripted joke. An amusing and sadistic little dig. Very funny.

"I apologise," said Bond. "Please continue." He gestured for Lucas to read on.

"On Monday the eighth of October, the defendant broke into another client's home address. This time, he savagely assaulted Mr Mick Miller, and forcefully inserted a large cucumber into his anus. The fact that the defendant discovered proof of Mr Miller's crime is neither here nor there, in my respectful submission. Mr Miller had to endure a surgical procedure to remove the cucumber and has been left with lasting damage to his rectum. Although Mr Chesterfield and Mr Miller were both subsequently convicted of their crimes, these vigilante attacks were illegal. Vigilantism is a crime."

"Indeed," said Bond. "Please... do enlighten me as to the events that transpired with Mr Chesterfield."

Lucas looked at the notes. Then he looked up at me.

"Mr Chesterfield hung himself two months into his prison sentence," he said.

Bradley leaned forward. "Your Honour..." he said, gesturing encouragement to Lucas. He wasn't asking. He was telling.

Lucas grimaced. "Your *Honour*," he said, begrudgingly.

And I had to admit... I hadn't known about Reginald Chesterfield. Not that I cared. I'd thoroughly expected it, even three years ago. But still...

Bond looked me up and down, with an exaggerated disgust. "Yes," he said. "Please continue."

* * *

I could feel blood now. I'd wriggled the ropes so much that I had probably caused a fair amount of injury to my wrists. Friction burns that had broken the skin. Not that I gave a shit. I couldn't feel it anyway, but it was definitely preferable to hanging.

The thing to do was to simultaneously stretch the rope *and* use the lubrication of my own blood to slide my wrists out. And it was coming. It wasn't far, either.

The best part was that not one of those two sadistic motherfuckers had a clue.

They'd seized my big psycho-knife. That was nowhere to be seen. But when Lucas clumped me over the back of the head, they'd obviously got me into the noose pretty sharpish.

They'd failed to search me properly and I could feel the little ceramic vegetable knife, stashed away in my vest. Lucas hadn't even known about it. I could feel its bulge, pressing against my ribs. And I wanted it. Knowing it was there, and knowing that they didn't know it was there, gave me a sense of drive.

When I got my hands on it, I was going to do some *serious* fucking cutting.

* * *

"The final element of this case," continued Lucas, "is the tragic murder of Mr Johnny Clayton. On the evening of Sunday the fourteenth of October, Mr Clayton was arrested on suspicion of burglary and sexual assault. Two offences for which…"

Lucas trailed off. He lowered the sheets of paper and I saw his eyes flick towards me, then back towards Bond.

"Is there a problem?" said Bradley. "You *did* come here to save those unfortunate women, did you not?"

I caught the guilty flicker again. Lucas raised the papers.

"Two offences for which Mr Clayton had a perfectly legitimate alibi, which the police were, of course, compelled to investigate. On Wednesday the seventeenth of October, the defendant broke into Mr Clayton's home address, tied him up and beat him. He then proceeded to torture Mr Clayton, using a blow-torch to inflict severe injuries upon his penis. During this incident, Mr Clayton's brother, who appears tonight in these court proceedings…"

Bradley gently waved.

"… attended Mr Clayton's house to find the defendant, in his vigilante costume, standing in front of Mr Clayton's unconscious body. He proceeded to engage the defendant in a reasonable display of threat, following which, the defendant managed to retrieve an empty needle and inject Mr Clayton with an air-bubble. The defendant's actions were not only illegal, they were based on the unproven belief that Mr Clayton had committed an offence he had not at that time been charged with. The defendant, despite pleading not guilty to these offences, was in the habit of leaving 'calling-cards' at the scenes of his vigilante attacks to identify his alter-ego, The Revengelist, as the perpetrator of these attacks. He used internet social networking sites to rally public support. Following these attacks, he went on to viciously assault Your Honour in the again unproven belief that you were involved in many allegations of perverting the course of justice, in relation to which no charges were ever made."

Lucas finished by screwing the pages up and throwing them down. "That, Your Honour, is the case for the prosecution."

* * *

Lucas hung his head in shame. Trouble was, he'd gone to the trouble of fucking me over enough to hand me over to these bastards. Reading all that bullshit wasn't going to make much difference, really. He couldn't have refused anyway. Certainly not considering Bond was threatening to let the women die if he did. He'd already done the dirty on me; all this… it was just making the dirt a little dirtier.

His primary objective had been to save the women. I knew that. We all fucking knew it. But the experience of shitting all over me might have been hard enough on its own. Rubbing my nose in it just made his own guilt worse.

"Well," said Bond, turning to Rachel. She was sitting cross-legged on the cold, hard ground in front of me. Her hands still tied behind her back. Her head was hung low, too. Her hair loose around her face. "You had better have a very good argument for your client, Miss Slater. I can assure you, his position is very dicey at the moment. Hanging, as you might say, by a thread."

Rachel made no effort to get up. And to be entirely honest, part of me wanted her to jump to her feet. To start shouting and bawling and making a big fuss. To demand my release and stop all this fucking around.

But she wouldn't do that. Under the circumstances, it was not the right thing to do.

"Miss Slater?" Bond's voice had the sharp edge of smugness. The obvious tones of gloating.

I *knew* that tone.

"The defence concedes. The case against the defendant is overwhelming," she said. Her voice was weak. It was full of defeat and anger and hate.

I felt a great sagging feeling. From this second on, there was only one thing that could be known for certain. Everyone in this room wanted me dead. And that, under the apparent circumstances, was right. It was *just*.

But it was just as well for me that the apparent circumstances were not the *actual* circumstances.

"Well," said Bond. "Then it only remains for me to deliver my verdict in this matter. Mr Clayton?"

Bradley stood to attention.

"Your Honour," he barked. "On the charges of burglary, assault, torture and murder relating to Mr Chesterfield, Mr Miller and Mr Clayton… have you reached a verdict?"

"Yes," said Bond. "Yes, I have."

"And how do you find the defendant on all charges, Your Honour?"

Bond looked right at me with hate in his soul, daggers in his eyes and a very grim desire to see me hang.

"*Guilty!*" he shouted.

* * *

Of course, the circumstances that Bond, Bradley, Lucas and Rachel thought that they were all so certain of were that I was standing on a wobbly chair with a noose around my neck. That my hands were tied tightly behind my back with rope. That I had no possible chance of escape whatsoever.

What I was certain of, however, was that thanks to my condition, and despite the very probable friction burns, cuts and the blood, I had managed to wriggle out of the ropes during Bond's little speech to Rachel about having a good argument to put forward in my defence.

From that point onwards, I was just biding my time. Waiting for the right moment.

And it was coming very soon.

* * *

"It now falls to this Court," said Bond, "to pass sentence. But before doing so, let the records show that the defendant is getting off lucky. True justice would see every injury he caused inflicted back upon him. But we are a civilised society, and the sentence of this Court is that the defendant will be hanged by the neck until dead. *Immediately!* Mr Clayton, if you don't mind."

Bradley stepped forward. "With pleasure, Your Honour."

He walked towards me. I couldn't see his face. The mask of Skull-Fuck, like the skeletal face of Death, was moving towards me instead. But beneath that mask, he was probably grinning from ear to ear. Enjoying every damn second of it.

And this… *this* was the moment.

* * *

It happened like this.

With my hands now free, I reached up and quickly pulled the noose over my head. Bradley clocked this, and although I couldn't see the look of shock on his face I was sure it was there. He quickened his pace and then broke into a sprint towards me as I jumped down off the chair. My hand went up to my stab-proof vest. Slipped inside. Retrieved the knife.

As Bradley saw the blade he skidded to sudden a halt. "What the f—"

I didn't let him finish. I lunged forward, taking full advantage of his shock. Grabbed him by the throat with one hand and with a super-speed double-stab I blinded him. One lightning-quick stab in each skeleton eye-socket. He screamed out with a shrill and piercing cry as blood squirted out of the eye-holes, flowing down the tracks of the red fake trickles he'd drawn on, and down the over-white plastic mask.

"*OH GOD MY EYES, OH JESUS GOD!!*"

Bradley sank to his knees, clutching at his face. Screaming and howling and crying.

I looked up. Bond had watched me free myself. Had risen to his feet, ready to run for it. Perhaps waiting to see for sure what I was going to do.

Lucas had seen me, too. He was pulling out his gun, although not necessarily to shoot me. It looked self-defensive, more than anything. Just arming himself in readiness for *something*.

Rachel was also aware of my bid for freedom. She was looking up at me.

They *all* wore the expression of surprise and dismay. *What did this mean?* they were probably thinking. *Were the women going to die? Had I fucked it all up to save myself?*

No. Not if I had anything to do with it.

I stepped towards Bond. I saw him flinch in readiness to make a getaway.

"Where are they?" I said. "Where are you holding the women, you ugly cunt?"

He stepped backwards. His eyes darted from left to right. His mind would be awash with panic. Thoughts of escape.

"Please… don't hurt me," he said.

"You saw what I just did to *that* fucker? Tell me where the women are!"

I saw Lucas raise the gun and for a moment I thought he was going to point it at me. My paranoia flared up. I didn't like guns, and from experience I didn't like the feeling of having one pointed at me. But I saw him aim the gun at Bond, instead.

Now we outnumbered him.

"Please don't point that gun at me," he whimpered. "Don't hurt me. I'll do anything you want."

"Then tell me where the women are!"

"I don't know what women you're talking about!" yelled Bond. There was a desperate and terrified shriek in his voice.

Something wasn't right.

"Please don't hurt me again!"

I looked at Lucas. He looked back at me, frowning. He shrugged slightly.

I stepped toward him again and shouted at him. "Tell me now!"

Bond sank to his knees. "*Help me!*" he screamed.

And a moment later, I heard the distant sirens.

* * *

"Oh shit!" I said.

I looked at Lucas. Then at Rachel. There was fear in their eyes. Worry and concern.

All of a sudden, Bond started making that horrible raspy hacking sound. That bronchial, barking laugh. I turned. Looked at him.

He was still kneeling, but he was looking right at me now. That hideous grin of his looked somehow more menacing. A terrible glint of smugness in his eyes. I saw him reach out a hand, his fist closed around something. He turned it over flat, facing upwards. Uncurled his fingers. Then he looked down at the object I could now see in his palm.

It was a mobile phone. He was recording us, the twat. He'd obviously set this up in advance. Tipped off the police himself, and told them to be here by a certain time. The only thing he hadn't planned for was me breaking free and getting stabby. And whilst that didn't bode well for his plan to hang me, it didn't necessarily bode well for my plan to get the fuck out of here.

He looked up from the phone. Up into my eyes.

"You lose, Jack," he said.

The sirens were getting closer.

* * *

Okay. Stay calm. If there was one thing I needed to do, it was stay calm.

My emotional response to this situation was anger. Fear. But of all the moments in my life when I couldn't allow my emotions to take control of my thought process, it was now. This wasn't going to pan out the way I had hoped, and I just had to accept that.

The women, however, had to be saved.

So, stay calm.

I looked back at Bond. I nodded and when I spoke, I spoke gently.

"Where are they, Rupert?"

He relished this moment. I saw it in the way he looked away from me languidly and down at the floor. "The cellar," he said. "But it won't do you any good. The police will be here any minute."

I nodded again. "I know," I said. "Lucas, you should go and get them."

Lucas made a dash for the door. "On it!" he said.

Bond was still staring at me. "You can beat me now, if you want."

"I *do* want," I said.

"Jack, don't!" Rachel's voice carried a desperate plea upon it.

I smiled. "But I'm not going to," I said, looking back at Bond. "Because it's what you *want* me to do."

The sirens were louder, now. Within a few moments, they were right outside the Old Courthouse. I could see blue flashing lights through a window. I could hear commotion and shouting.

It didn't take long for the courtroom to fill up with armed coppers.

Eleven

The duty solicitor was some guy called Jeffrey Cooper. He worked for one of Robert Mitchell's biggest rivals and although I didn't know him personally, he seemed like a decent enough lawyer.

After being taken into custody, I was booked in by Sgt Hardwick, of all fuckers. There was little in the way of pleasantries. His interactions were distant and formal. I requested the duty solicitor, cooperated with the booking-in procedure and bedded down for the night in a cell.

The following morning I ate some toast, brought to me by a civilian detention officer. A cup of rubbish coffee from a vending machine. In the early part of the afternoon, I discovered that my solicitor had turned up and wanted to see me.

I shuffled out of the cell, wearing a blue paper 'onesie' given to me after all my Revengelist clobber was seized for evidential purposes. No doubt forensics were crawling all over it with a fine-tooth comb. They wouldn't find anything, of course. I already knew that.

Furthermore, I knew that not only was Reginald Chesterfield dead, Mick Miller was serving a stretch inside for the rape of that young model. Even if he wanted to provide a statement to the police about The Revengelist, there was no evidence from the cucumber incident that connected me to it.

Johnny Clayton's murder was dicier ground. Bradley had been able to find out from Claire Edwards that I *was* The Revengelist. She'd seen me, and heard my name. Furthermore, she'd discussed the matter with Rodney Lucas before leaving him. The question here was whether Lucas and his wife would make statements against me, because if they didn't, there was no evidence linking me to the Revengelist.

So, where did that leave me?

Well, as far as Mum was concerned, again, the only people who knew I'd killed her were the Lucas family. Possibly Frank, but he'd never really made it clear one way or the other. The fact that no one took his claims I was The Revengelist seriously, though, was a good starting point.

Bradley Clayton was totally fucked. At such time that the abducted women were all questioned – and it would have to be done when they were well enough, carefully and sensitively – they'd all implicate Bradley for sure. He was the only one they'd seen, which was no doubt why Bond got him involved. He stood little chance. The fact that he was suffering some very serious injuries was neither here nor there as far as the investigating officers were concerned. He'd be at hospital now, being treated for his stab wounds, but under careful guard of his arresting officers.

Bond, however, was a different story. None of the women, besides Rachel, had known of his connection to the kidnappings. But if Rachel started filling in the blanks, the police would start piecing together why we were all there in the Old Courthouse. Why there was a noose hanging from the ceiling. A cellar filled with half-starved, kidnapped women. Why ex-DCI Lucas was there with a firearm. And why I was wearing an outfit that closely resembled the outfit worn by the criminal known as The Revengelist.

So, in order to save my arse, Bond must not be implicated.

It was an awful, and ultimately, very complicated mess.

And before Jeffrey sat me down to enlighten me about all the information he'd been given by way of pre-interview disclosure, I was very tempted indeed to just put my hands up to it all. To throw in the towel and cough to everything.

* * *

But that would have been a silly mistake.

Jeffrey took me through the evidence as disclosed to him by the investigating officers. And at that stage, neither Lucas nor Rachel had made a statement, and Claire Edwards – like the other women – was just too shaken up. The evidence that Jeffrey disclosed immediately revealed the gaping holes in the police case.

My mind worked quickly and efficiently, drawing on my experience as an expert in criminal law. Cobbling together a plausible account that took advantage of the weaknesses in the evidence. And that was how, several hours later, I was bailed from the police station pending further police enquiries.

It was also how Bond walked free.

* * *

As I stepped out of the police station and onto the street, I took a good breath of air. I glanced around and saw Rachel sitting on a bench on the opposite side of the road.

Our eyes met and stayed locked.

I reached up and tugged on the collar of the coat I was wearing. The clothes that she had given to the custody staff for me to wear on my release. I nodded to her, smiling.

She smiled back.

We couldn't be seen talking. Not yet. And definitely not *here*. If anyone was watching, it might look suspicious.

There was a look of concern etched on her features. But the sun was shining on this fresh autumn afternoon. It wasn't warm. There was a slight chill, actually, but it was nice. I had planned to get a cab and retrieve the Mustang, which was parked a couple of streets away from the Old Courthouse. But I decided to walk, instead. Liberty is one of those things you take for granted. When you've just spent the night in a police cell, you appreciate the outdoor air a bit more.

I dipped my head to her, in a "thank you" nod and she promptly returned it.

And then I walked off, disappearing into the crowds of everyday folk going about their daily business.

* * *

Over the course of the following weeks I couldn't help wondering whether it was right that Rupert Bond had gone free. Would Rachel and Lucas make statements against him? Would they see justice done and ensure that he went down, taking me with him? Whilst it was true that for the time being I was on police bail, something didn't seem right about that bastard not being brought to justice.

But I went about my life without bothering anyone. Kept my nose clean. Did my best to stay out of trouble. And then one day, I got a letter in the post.

It was from Rachel.

Dear Jack,

Lucas and his wife got back together. I wasn't sure whether you'd heard, but I thought you'd like to know that. I'm going for a job in victim support. I think I'll be better suited to it.

Lucas says he has "very good reason" to believe the CPS will not charge you. As far as historical matters are concerned, there's just no evidence. A certain number of KEY WITNESSES haven't come forward to make statements. He also says to tell you not to worry about Bond. Bond won't be saying a thing. Of that, he says, you can be sure.

Lastly, I wanted to thank you for coming to my rescue. I owe you a lot, but the only thing I can give you is honesty. So here it is:

This will be the last time you ever hear from me. You saved my life, and it is a debt I cannot repay. But I cannot see you again. Ever. I know that you will understand why.

All the best,

Rachel.

PS: I hardly need to explain why, but please destroy this letter.

* * *

I burned it immediately. I didn't want anything coming back on her.

And in the end, she was right. I wasn't charged with a damn thing. As Rachel pointed out, there wasn't a single piece of evidence to pin me down as The Revengelist. Lucas, his wife *and* Rachel had all refused to give a statement.

During my police interview, I'd told the police that Bradley was the brother of my ex-client Johnny Clayton, and that he'd become obsessed with the idea that I was The Revengelist, although I didn't know why and he had no evidence to substantiate his claim, anyway. I said that, somehow, he found out where I lived and harassed me for months, claiming that he would "out" me as the vigilante. In the end, I said, he resorted to trying to frame me.

I told them that I was *also* one of the kidnapping victims. I was taken after working late one night, walking back to my car. I explained that I'd woken at one point during my ordeal to find myself bound, and strung up by the neck in a fake Revengelist costume. That during the pretend and thoroughly fixed trial that followed, I managed to escape and the only way of stopping him was to use force.

It looked as though the police had little choice but to accept this explanation.

And a few days after receiving Rachel's letter, I happened upon this article in the news.

BODY OF LAWYER FOUND
Police Appeal for Witnesses

The body of criminal defence lawyer, Rupert Bond, formerly of Bond, Jenkins & Coleridge Solicitors, was found yesterday by a local man whilst out walking his dog. Police confirm that the body showed signs of having been strangled and dumped in a skip that was being used for the clearance of the Old Courthouse, a disused Victorian magistrates' court that Mr Bond himself owned...

As I read the report, I smiled to myself. Justice *had* been served.

Last Words, MotherFucker!

In the days that followed, I often found myself thinking back to the graffiti I'd seen in the Old Courthouse.

> *No such thing as crime. No such thing as justice.*
> *There's only action and revenge.*

I'd always thought that graffiti artists were just bored-shitless yobs with spray-paint, slashing their names across any available brick-wall surface like chimps flinging handfuls of their own shit around.

But what about people like Banksy? They had something *worth* saying, and they did it in a way you could hardly ignore. That piece of graffiti in the pissy Courthouse hallway was *philosophy*. It was intelligent and reasoned thought, conveyed by a means of a communication that would appeal to those who hadn't been made homeless with their library of 20th century philosophy in tow.

Criminal laws were not an objective standard of human behaviour. Crime is simply behaviour that is prohibited by people in charge of society, on *behalf* of society. And considering that laws *change* over time, what society once considered a crime in the past might not be considered a crime now.

Consider the fact that homosexuality was once a crime.

Consider Heresy.

Consider the paintings you've seen depicting people burned at the stake. People slaughtered because they spoke out against religion.

I mean… religion, for Christ's sake! Was it worth *murdering* people for?

Sure, people claim that they have spoken to God. Indeed, some people make a good living from it. But people also claim to have spoken to ghosts, time travellers and aliens.

Anyone who says they've had an alien probe shoved up their arse is surely no more a suitable candidate for sectioning than someone who says they can communicate with a being in the sky who built the world in six days. The fact that religion has infiltrated social conditioning to the extent that it has seems to afford it a certain disproportionate clout. Blasphemy seeks to control what people say about a system of beliefs that is highly susceptible to criticism. There's no such thing as crime, in exactly the same way that there is no such thing as blasphemy. It's all just a matter of perspective, and the rules made up to defend that perspective. The difference, I think, is the degree to which such thinking pervades our consciousness.

Take blasphemy… If I told a UFO nut that aliens don't exist and that if they did exist, they're sadistic cunts, how is that more acceptable than saying that God does not exist and, if He did exist, is *also* a sadistic cunt? Is the offence that *one* group takes more important than the offence that *another* group takes?

The piece of graffiti in that hallway was reminding us that society clubs together. It agrees on a set of rules that should enable *all* to flourish. And when those rules are broken, punishments are part of the package. But these rules are simply that… a meeting of minds. An agreement by people in charge, which is enforced to impose control.

Most modern laws stem in some way or other from the beliefs of Christianity. Nietzsche argued that Christianity developed back when the brutality of the Roman Empire gave rise to persecution, and such a belief system was – arguably – the means by which the persecution could justifiably be considered 'evil'. If you find yourself able to grasp *this*, and able to then consider things as though stepping *beyond* and *outside* of it all, you can see that no matter what any law says, it isn't actually wrong or evil to behave in any particular way. It only becomes perceived as such when enough people subscribe to it. Everything we condemn – every rotten act of human shittiness – throughout the *entire* course of history, is condemned only with the unshakable influence of a lifetime – of *generations* even – of deep-reaching conditioning.

Shaking off beliefs you've grown up with your whole life is hard. Two thousand years of an all-pervading moral blueprint is even harder. And they say that justice is about balance. But justice, really, is nothing more than a concept of socially acceptable revenge.

* * *

So, where did The Revengelist fit into all this?

Well, I'm a product of social conditioning just the same as everyone else. I can *understand* this, and I can take pride and pleasure in knowing that I understand this, but I can't change it. Not on my own, anyway. And I'm not entirely sure I would want to.

I'm not saying that the existence of this particular moral code is wrong, and anyway, we've evolved too far now to try and just flip it overnight to see what happens. We've awarded ourselves fundamental rights, and it seems quite fair to do so. Those rights certainly could not be easily withdrawn from us. Not without a serious fucking fight, anyway.

Remember the list I made? The seven simple facts behind human nature?

1) People are taught from an early age to value self-worth.

2) Self-worth becomes the motivation for self-improvement.

3) Self-worth and self-improvement form the determination to survive. To value the existence of the self, and to form the central "right" to not be prevented from existing or achieving self-improvement.

4) The understanding that all others possess the same values.

5) The understanding that all others therefore pose a potential risk, in possessing those same values, to your own values.

6) The mistrust of others at a deep and fundamental level.

7) The devaluing of others' values in relation to our own.

This list shows why human beings are capable of being so horrible, and it also proves that criminal laws are indeed essential, certainly for the foreseeable future. Certainly, until human beings achieve some sort of intellectual enlightenment. And that's fine by me. At the moment, we're all still children, fighting and squabbling and playing at being civilised. People understand the existence of the rights we've given ourselves, and they understand that in order to ensure they prevail, laws have to be put in place.

But because of this list, and because we're all still fucking children, we still come back to the same problem. The problem which says that what one person thinks is justice, another person might not. Seeking balance for say, a murder, can involve different things depending on where in the world you may be. Life-imprisonment, or the lethal injection.

Which one is right?

Well, that's something we can't answer so easily, because it depends on your perspective. It all depends on what is considered right for a particular society.

Think about this: Imagine a tribe of human beings somewhere, living undiscovered, deep within unexplored territory. Untouched by outsiders. Unsullied by our beliefs.

A tribe that didn't consider the killing of another human being in quite the same way we do? What if they didn't *punish* this act? What if it had some different sequence of repercussions, like promotion in the ranks, the assimilation of property?

Those are the reasons justice is hard to define, and hard to defend. You hear about idiots all the time bashing the fuck out of people they say have done them wrong. You hear about people wrongly accused of being a paedophile, say, and beaten to within an inch of their life, only to then be cleared of the original accusations. The beating may have seemed *just* at first. It may have seemed like a good idea to smash the face in of that rotten pervert a few doors down from where you live, but when he's cleared, it sheds a whole new light on the matter.

How the tables can quickly turn.

That's why you had to be smart about it. I only targeted my clients. If you go after people based on belief it's not good enough. You have to *know* that what you're doing is based on fact. I only went after people about whom I had knowledge that no one else did. People about whom I could make educated judgments. If I sometimes had to fill in the blanks, then so be it. I'm smart. I'm not some swaggering knucklehead.

If justice was therefore just a socially acceptable form of revenge, the question was this: Why should *my* revenge, *my* punishment be any less legitimate than society's?

So, no. Fuck Bond, and fuck Bradley Clayton. Fuck all of them. Fuck Reginald Chesterfield, Mick Miller, Johnny Clayton. And fuck Mum, Frank and Leon Hunt.

Fuck all of them! They *all* deserved what they got, because although it may not have been justice as society views justice, it was justice as *I* view it.

It was justice to *me.*

Besides, that was it now. I'd totally had enough of the whole thing. I quit. I quit being The Revengelist. No more.

Or… maybe, anyway. We'd see.

We'd just wait and see.

Lightning Source UK Ltd.
Milton Keynes UK
UKHW020645020120
356253UK00012B/712/P